"You went somev

Jamie stood up and
stared out the window and toward the lake. She
put her hand on his lower back, and the action and
warmth were so soft and unexpected that he tensed
for a moment before relaxing into her touch.

When he did, Jamie's face softened. "Are you okay?"

He nodded and turned to her. She kept her hand on
his back, and as he moved, she wrapped her other
arm around him as well. Her touch made his pulse
race.

He reached up and pushed a small strand of hair
from her face. "Do you have any idea how beautiful
you are?" He smiled at her as he looked into her
eyes.

"Thank you." Jamie grinned but didn't look away
coquettishly as some women would have done. She
was so strong. "I have to tell you, from the first time
I saw you on the mountain, I have been imagining
what a moment like this with you would feel like."

MYSTERY ON THE RANGE

DANICA WINTERS

Harlequin

INTRIGUE

For all of those who have never fit in, lean into what makes you different. It is what makes you awesomely you, and it is likely your greatest strength.

Acknowledgments

Thanks to Emma and Katarina, who put up with my manic schedules and crazy deadline races. You guys are the best. And I can't adequately express how grateful I am for such a great team at Harlequin—US and worldwide.

Also, thank you to Jill for making things happen.

Harlequin®
INTRIGUE™

Recycling programs for this product may not exist in your area.

ISBN-13: 978-1-335-69010-4

Mystery on the Range

Copyright © 2025 by Danica Winters

Harlequin Enterprises ULC
22 Adelaide St. West, 41st Floor
Toronto, Ontario M5H 4E3, Canada
www.Harlequin.com

Printed in Lithuania

MIX
Paper | Supporting responsible forestry
FSC® C021394

Danica Winters is a multiple-award-winning, bestselling author who writes books that grip readers with their ability to drive emotion through suspense and occasionally a touch of magic. When she's not working, she can be found in the wilds of Montana, testing her patience while she tries to hone her skills at various crafts—quilting, pottery and painting are not her areas of expertise. She believes the cup is neither half-full nor half-empty, but it better be filled with wine. Visit her website at danicawinters.net.

Books by Danica Winters

Harlequin Intrigue

West Glacier Ranch Suspense

Rodeo Crime Ring
Mystery on the Range

Big Sky Search and Rescue

Helicopter Rescue
Swiftwater Enemies
Mountain Abduction
Winter Warning

STEALTH: Shadow Team

A Loaded Question
Rescue Mission: Secret Child
A Judge's Secrets
K-9 Recovery
Lone Wolf Bounty Hunter
Montana Wilderness Pursuit

Stealth

Hidden Truth
In His Sights
Her Assassin For Hire
Protective Operation

Visit the Author Profile page at Harlequin.com.

CAST OF CHARACTERS

Jamie Trapper—A retired barrel-racing cowgirl who is running from the traumas of her past and straight into the horrors that she must confront in her present in order to have a healthy future.

Pierce Hauser—A sexy park ranger for Glacier National Park who must work fast to solve a series of attacks before anyone else gets hurt.

Vince Sanford—Pierce's best friend and coworker, but also a man who has more than his fair share of skeletons in his closet.

Patrol Captain Eliot Reynolds—A man imprisoned by his secrets but set free by his job.

Nicole Reynolds—Eliot's wife and the woman behind the man...and maybe the one who is really running the show.

Carey Donovan—The catty wife of the murdered mayor who everyone loves to hate.

Mayor Clyde Donovan—The infamously crooked mayor of the local small town who has been missing for years until his remains are unearthed in Glacier National Park.

Prologue

The man's screams pierced the evening air. The wails of pain and terror echoed across the glacial moraines of the park and crashed down on her, making the hairs on Jamie Trapper's arms rise.

She'd never heard a sound like it before, but she held no doubts that it was the call of a dying man.

She hadn't brought a gun, and she knew her best friend Matt Goldstock hadn't, either, but she instinctively looked to his hip as he stopped ahead of her on the dirt trail leading to Avalanche Lake.

"What in the world was that?" Matt asked, turning toward her.

Matt was a good man, but not well versed in the ways of the wilderness, especially not an area rife with dangerous predators—both of the four- and two-legged varieties.

"That means we need to run." She cinched her backpack tighter and took off in a full sprint toward the sound as the man cried out again.

She found strength in the fact he was still making the strong, haunting sound. If he was fighting, he was still alive.

Her footfalls crunched in the gravel of the trail as she moved as fast as her body would allow. She hadn't moved this quickly since...*that night.* She couldn't think about that now. No. She shook the thoughts of John away.

There was a strange, animalistic scream in the dusk and the man's cry followed, but it was muted, warbling. They were locked in battle. Man versus beast.

If she had to guess, beast was winning.

She sent out a silent bid for the man to persevere and push through, to summon the power and animalistic nature within him to come out on top—or at least continue to survive.

She pushed herself harder.

Matt brushed by her and she tried to keep pace. Her lungs ached as she pushed up the mountain as the elevation grew exponentially. She'd spent too many days in the flatlands rodeoing and it was catching up with her.

It angered her she couldn't catch Matt, but she wasn't about to tell him to slow down when a man's life hung in the balance.

Matt's foot slipped in the gravel and he grabbed an exposed root to steady himself.

"Are you okay?" she asked between heavy breaths as she caught up.

He nodded but he was gasping for breath. "Go."

She drove forward. Pushing over the crest of the gain in the trail, something flashed across the path in front of her. In the thin light, all she saw was a dark mass that she could identify as animal and nothing more.

Ahead of her, amid torn-up dirt and a smattering of blood, was a man.

His clothes were ripped, and blood gushed from his forehead and down his face. "Matt!" She screamed. "Matt! Get help!"

She unclicked her pack and dropped it to the ground beside the man, pulling out her emergency medical kit.

There was so much blood on his face and clothing that it looked as if he had bathed in red. Even his khaki hiking pants were nearly covered. It appeared as if the animal had mostly attacked his upper body, head and neck area, but without pulling back his shirt, she couldn't be sure.

Matt moved beside her. "Let me do this." He gave her a knowing look as he pressed his fingers against the man's neck and checked his vital signs. "Don't worry, he's still alive. For now."

She hadn't noticed how badly her hands were shaking until he motioned toward them. That was new. She'd been so good in emergencies until Wyoming.

Until Wyoming.

It was humbling how a person's entire existence could change when a solitary haunting moment was consumed by tragedy.

Chapter One

Being stalked by a mountain lion was like a failing relationship: a person rarely saw the deathblow coming. And man, oh man, had Pierce missed the signs that his breakup was imminent.

Even though it had been six months since his ex, Haven Andrus, had called off their engagement, he was still fielding calls about what was supposed to have been their wedding date this week. He laid the phone down, just having acknowledged the latest unprovoked attack via text message from his great-aunt Kim who had, for some unknown reason, decided it was a great idea to reach out with condolences.

He hadn't needed the reminder that today was supposed to be his rehearsal dinner.

Yes, he was glad his cousin had set a reminder in her mother's phone—but it would have been even better if she had remembered to delete the stupid thing. It would have saved Pierce the salt in the wound.

As if saying a clipped "Thanks" didn't make it clear enough that Pierce didn't want to delve into the emotions and pain that filled this week, his phone pinged again with another message from his aunt. This time he ignored it. He couldn't handle chatting. Emotions weren't his strong suit, and his aunt was far too much like all the women in their family—they just wanted to pick apart anything and everything that involved feelings until all that was left on the ground were bones.

Though today was supposed to be his day off from work as a ranger at Glacier National Park, he'd picked up a shift for his friend Vince Sanford. The worst part was that Vince had taken the days off to be his best man. He had offered to take Pierce anywhere he wanted for the week, but the last thing Pierce had needed was to have more free time to think.

He needed to run a chainsaw and pick up logs until his fingers were raw and torn beneath the fingertips of his gloves and sweat pooled at the base of his throat. Better, he needed to pound at the earth with a pickax and shovel— to tear and gnaw at the dirt like it was the feelings that he needed to turn to dust and bury.

Yes, work would keep him busy and be the catharsis he needed so desperately—especially at Glacier. This summer they were expecting to host at least three million visitors. Those kinds of numbers brought big-city problems to the backcountry of Montana. To cap it off, many tourists expected the amenities of cities but were instead faced with narrow winding roads, the realities of winter weather in summer months, predatory animals, elevation sickness and the unpredictability of nature. Usually, that meant he had all kinds of shenanigans to deal with.

At least as a federal employee he had a lot of freedom in his job. Today, he was running the southern boundary of the park near Apgar. Last week, he'd been working up north near Polebridge. He wished he was back there; up north there were fewer people and the residents who lived there year-round were some of the quirkiest around. His favorite townie was a woman named Poppy, who had a two-hundred-pound gray wolf named Luna she walked through the center of the one-laned town every day. Sometimes Luna even wore a little bone in her hair.

There was a rumor Poppy had found Luna in an abandoned wolf's den after the mother wolf had been hit by a tourist's car. Luna had been the only cub that had survived. There was also another take on the tale that she had stolen the pup from a wolf den. The latest he'd heard was far less entertaining: Poppy had merely bought the pup from a dealer near Missoula.

He liked to think Poppy had been doing something philanthropic—even if it was something he could write her a ticket for doing. In a small town, where he needed folks to be his friend and allies, it often worked to his advantage to turn a blind eye. Luna was happy and well-kept, and Poppy loved her immensely and didn't put humans or the wolf in any situation where either could be hurt. So, if she had saved the wolf pup from starvation, he was okay with how things had turned out. Plus, it was nice seeing the pair.

He drove around the long, snaking line of cars that was barely moving as the tourists poured out of the gates near West Glacier. He gave Lloyd, his favorite gatekeeper and park employee, a wave as he drove through the entry gates and made his way inside the park.

Apgar was just closing for the day and the doors to the markets were half shut and waiting for the last straggling customers to leave. Soon the bells on the doors would stop constantly dinging with the comings and goings of the visitors purchasing little mountain goat magnets, Sasquatch playing cards and T-shirts with *Glacier* printed across the backs.

Oh, and he couldn't forget the bear spray. Everyone would drop forty dollars on a can of bear spray that they would throw away at the end of their trip. Several local kids had learned they could hit the garbage cans both outside the airport and inside the park, when the maintenance crews weren't around, to find unused bear sprays they could re-sell outside the gates of the park for twenty bucks. They made a killer profit, from what he could tell—they always had a line.

He couldn't begrudge their hustle. If the local kids wanted to benefit from the constant barrage of guests, kudos to them. If anything, he just wished that they'd had bear spray to sell when he'd been a kid so he could have run the same hustle. It really was brilliant.

His phone pinged several times with a series of messages as he neared the main ranger's headquarters. The building was new—well at least by the park's standards, having been built in the early 2000s—and it had been kept in the style of the other chestnut-brown-painted log buildings that adorned the village. Its windows were framed in white, which it gave it a quaint charm. In fact, it was so charming and in line with the other buildings of the town that no one ever noticed it was tucked back behind the shops—they'd hidden it perfectly in plain sight.

As he pulled into his designated parking spot, his phone pinged. He glanced at the message.

There had been an attack. Any and all available rangers were to report. Normally, as a National Park Service Special Agent, he would just handle matters affiliated with law enforcement, but according to the GPS on his computer in his truck, he was the nearest available responder.

According to Dispatch, the animal attack had happened close to Avalanche Lake. From the GPS coordinates they'd sent him, it was about two miles up the trail. Little was known except the man attacked had been alone at the time of the event and, at the time of the call, was still alive. The hikers who had found him were with him now and awaiting help.

He typed a quick message to Dispatch, letting them know he was taking the call and advising them to notify Two Bear Air that they would need an airlift for the victim to Logan Medical Health Center in Kalispell.

He pulled out of his spot at headquarters and sped through the town, turning on his lights and sirens. He weaved between cars and made his way down the road toward Avalanche Lake. It normally took thirty minutes to get there for the average driver, but he could do it in fifteen.

Without a doubt, he would beat the life-flight helicopter. He would have to sprint up the mountain to reach the victim and get him stabilized and ready for flight before their arrival.

As he raced down the road, he did a mental checklist, going through all the items in his kit, and what he would do when he arrived. If the man was as bad off as Pierce assumed, he would be lucky to be alive. Big cats loved to go after the neck, and they normally attacked from behind. If it was a bear attack, it was probably a grizzly that had gotten a hold of him. In which case, it was good there were other people with him as the animal was likely to come back and finish the kill.

Either way, the man was likely bleeding profusely and

would need a high level of care. He would have to get it under control before he could make any moves.

It took fourteen minutes and forty-two seconds to arrive on scene. It was a personal best. When he pulled up to the trailhead, there was nowhere to park, but he pulled to a stop blocking the main gate. The visitors to the park could work around him.

He grabbed his medic's bag and rushed out onto the trail. As he jogged up the winding trail, his boots clacked on the wooden boards until he hit the dirt. The trail was a beautiful one, and normally he enjoyed taking his out-of-state friends on the well-groomed path to the crystal-blue lake fed by waterfalls. Yet today he barely noticed the pines as he ran through them and past the babbling creek.

He checked his phone. Two Bear was still on the ground and wouldn't be taking off for at least twenty more minutes as they were waiting on their flight crew. They wouldn't be on scene for another forty-five minutes, at least.

If the victim was down where Pierce assumed he was, there wasn't a location where the helicopter could land. They would have to run lines to him, and they would have to airlift the man out.

It would be a tricky save.

Nothing about this call was going to be easy.

As he twisted through the first mile or so, his lungs started to fight. It wasn't a huge elevation gain, but running with gear was tough. His thighs and calves burned. He just needed to get past the initial pain. It was unusual, but he loved that feeling, that pull from his body telling him to stop and yield to the ache. It was powerful to keep going, to take control and refuse to quit.

Rounding a corner, he nearly ran into a couple who were

wide-eyed with shock. The woman put her hands up in panic. "There's a man…" She pointed in the opposite direction. "That way…"

"He's not doing good." The man, who was wearing high-end hiking clothes, finished her sentence.

"But he's still alive?" Pierce asked.

The man nodded.

"How much farther?" he asked.

"Quarter mile," the man said as he and the woman he was with stepped to the side of the dirt trail to let him by.

He nodded as he ran past them. "Thanks," he said, trying to hide the fact that he was winded by his run.

The woman had been terrified by what she had witnessed, so much so that she and the man she was with had left the scene. That in and of itself was strange. Most people stayed to witness the turmoil unfolding, classic rubbernecking. Bystanders were common and, in situations like these in the woods, they could even be extremely helpful.

Checking his breathing, Pierce sped up. If the man was only another quarter of a mile or so ahead, he wasn't as far in as the GPS coordinates he'd been given, and he was grateful.

The smell of the attack hit him first; it was strong with the ripped earth, decaying pine needles and the metallic scent of blood.

He hated that smell.

The last time he'd come across a scene like this had been on a call to an unwitnessed death by Logan Pass, where a woman had taken her own life at the base of a tree overlooking a glacial moraine. It was a memory that regularly haunted his thoughts.

Pierce turned the corner and came into a small opening.

Blood was splattered over the bunchgrass and smeared on the ponderosa pine nearest him. It was far worse than the woman's self-inflicted gunshot wound. There were masses of overturned dirt where there must have been a fight for survival.

It looked like a murder scene. From the volume of blood around the space, he found it hard to believe the man was still alive.

Moving carefully through the area, he came over the small hill and found a man with his back to him, staring down at the ground. He was wearing a Western-styled, red-plaid shirt and Wrangler jeans. Odd clothing for hiking, but he'd seen stranger. The man didn't seem to hear him as he approached.

Crouching beside the victim was a blond woman.

Pierce slowed down and tried to catch his breath. He didn't want to bring any additional stress to the situation. He had to be calm, cool and collected.

"Hey, guys," he said, trying to catch his breath. "My name is Pierce Hauser. I'm a ranger here at Glacier Park. I'm here to help."

The woman squatting beside the cowboy turned and looked up at him with vibrant blue eyes and gave him an appreciative nod of welcome.

The cowboy turned. "Glad to see ya." His face was stoic. If Pierce had to guess, the guy had seen trauma before. "We did what we could to try and stop the bleeding. He's doin' better now, but his pulse is getting' darn slow." He motioned toward the crouching woman.

From where he was standing, all he could see was the man's bloodied leather hiking boots. One of the boots was off and lying next to his socked foot in the middle of the trail. The cowboy stepped out of the way. The victim came fully into view.

Pierce walked over, trying not to stare at the woman who was wiping some of the blood from the man's face with a wet bandana. She was cooing soft words to the man, telling him he was going to be all right. Pierce appreciated her attempts to mollify the victim, but she had to know just as well as he did that with this amount of blood loss death was a real possibility.

The woman looked up at him with those striking eyes. Her eyes were the same crystal blue color as Avalanche Lake. Yet they looked far more haunted thanks to the scene around them. "His blood pressure is low. If we don't get him out of here soon, I don't think he's going to make it."

He nodded. "A helicopter is on the way. They'll be here soon. It looks like you have done a fantastic job getting him stabilized. What's your name?"

"Jamie... Jamie Trapper."

"Jamie, do you mind if I get in there and take his pulse?"

He motioned for him to take her position and she stood up and moved away from the man. As she stepped back, she exhaled with what he took to be relief.

He could understand the feeling, he knew it only too well.

The man's face was beyond recognition. There were lacerations across his nose and cheek, and he may have lost his left eye. It was hard to tell due to the swelling around the socket and all that was damaged.

Jamie had done a nice job cleaning up the excess blood and dabbing at the wounds, but they were still seeping blood. The fact that there was seepage was good—dead men didn't bleed.

"Does anybody know his name?" He squatted down beside the man and took his sluggish pulse, realizing he was dangerously bradycardic. "Has he been conscious at all since anybody arrived on scene?"

"We don't know his name. And, he hasn't woken up. Sorry. I tried to get him to come to, but we got nothing." Jamie shook her head, her blond hair falling loose from behind her ear where she had tucked it. She pushed it back, her action almost angry, like her hair had done something wrong by breaking free in such a moment.

They had placed a polyester belt around the man's thigh and wrapped it tight with a stick. The tourniquet was high and perfectly placed on the femoral artery. The woman had known what she was doing. Farther down the man's leg was a large gash in his jeans. They were nearly black with blood. He pulled the fabric back, exposing four smooth lacerations on the man's thigh.

Just below the lacerations was a bite mark. Two large canines, not far apart. From the looks of it, a mountain lion had been behind the attack.

He sucked in a breath. This event was about to become a major problem. Not only was the news of this attack going to be blasted across the papers, but they were going to have to deal with the fallout. Every action he took, or didn't take, was going to come under scrutiny. His butt was going to be on the line.

Plus, they were about to have a wave of panic throughout the park.

Cats rarely attacked people, but when they did, they didn't do it just once. When they started attacking humans, it meant they were desperate, and desperation only meant heightened danger.

Chapter Two

Jamie stared at the blood on her hands as she stood beside the creek before bending down to wash them. It was hardly the first time her hands had been covered in blood, but the last time she had promised herself she'd never be in that kind of situation again. That was what she got for saying *never*.

However, there was no way she and Matt could have ignored the man lying in the trail. It hadn't taken long for the helicopter to drop the line to the ranger and airlift the injured man out. And, as soon as he was gone, and the helicopter's thumping blades grew faint in the distance, it was almost as if nothing had happened. Silence returned. There was simply the sounds of forest animals and the babbling water. The only evidence of chaos was the blood.

She'd spent so many days on the rodeo circuit across the US that she'd seen all kinds of injuries—everything from goring to men crushed under trailers.

The last time she'd seen an injury this bad had been when her former boyfriend had gotten pinned under a bull six months ago. She could still smell the arena dirt in the air. When she'd gone to sleep that night, the collective sound of the crowd's gasp had haunted her dreams. That horrible night, she had moved over that fence and run to

his side before the bull had even been pushed back to the
pens by the clowns, but she hadn't cared.

The only thing she had thought about at that moment
was John.

She'd known the moment the bull had landed on him
what the outcome would be. The gray Brahman was one
of the largest bulls she had ever seen, well over a ton. Even
though John was wearing all the protective gear, there was
little it could do to protect a man from that kind of impact
to the head.

He had died instantly, but she had held him in her arms
until the paramedics had forced her to let him go.

She'd tried to remain on the rodeo circuit. It was what
John would have wanted her to do, but she had lost her taste
for it after he'd gotten killed. Whenever Matt went out, all
she could think about was John. Matt had been John's best
friend, too.

Matt was married to a woman named Sally, out of Juneau, and they rarely saw each other, but he was faithful,
and Jamie loved him for his loyalty. Ever since John's death,
Jamie had been traveling with Matt, and he'd supported
her when she'd told him she wanted to go back to Montana and to her family's ranch after her father and brother
had been found dead.

Thankfully, her brother Cameron had welcomed her with
open arms. He had put her up in the main house and even
given her and Matt jobs with the horses and cattle. She appreciated all he'd done for her when he could have just as
easily told her to pound sand after she had been away from
the ranch for so long. He had even gone as far as to give her
a cut of the property even though she hadn't been named
in their father's will. Leonard had always been the kind of

man who'd valued a son over a daughter, so when she had heard she and her sister had been left out, she hadn't really been surprised.

She also hadn't been heartbroken when she'd heard about her father's death or surprised by the circumstances that surrounded it.

"Are you okay?" A man's voice pulled her from her thoughts.

She had no idea how long she had been standing at the side of the creek looking from her fingers to the bubbling blue water as it rushed down the purple rocks and splashed and pooled in the holes and eddies created by hundreds of years of floods and droughts.

She turned to see the ranger standing behind her. His dark hair was closely cropped, and his ranger's uniform was unmarred. She glanced down at her own clothing. Her T-shirt was covered in the stranger's blood, as were the knees of her jeans. He probably wondered why she was hiking in jeans, but he could wonder all he wanted. At least she had swapped out her Tony Lamas for a pair of hiking boots. Few things could get her out of her cowboy boots.

"Jamie?" he asked, reaching over and touching her arm.

She jerked away from his hand. "Sorry," she said, instantly regretting her action. "You're fine touching me... I... You just caught me off guard." She reached over and touched his arm, but he frowned at her fingers and she let them drift off his brown shirt and her hand fell to her side.

"Are you doing okay?" he repeated.

He looked over at the place where the man had been lying. There was a flat spot in the shape of a coffin where the board had pressed into the dirt.

"I'm fine. This just brought up some things I thought I had dealt with, that's all."

"Ah, I see." He nodded. "This kind of thing has a way of doing that. When I first became a special agent, I didn't realize one of my primary jobs would be working as a paramedic."

"Is it really?" She'd had no idea.

He pinched his lips like he hated the idea but had resigned himself to his reality. "Yeah. More often than not, I'm the first responder. This time, unfortunately, it was you. However, you did an excellent job and everything that I could've done. You should be proud of yourself. You saved that man's life."

"Did you find out what his name was?" she asked.

"His ID said Anthony Lewis."

She glanced up at the sky where the blue helicopter had disappeared. Matt was sitting down on a large pine, tapping away on the Garmin GPS and messaging device, probably letting Sally know he was at least safe.

"You and I both know that Anthony isn't out of the woods. He may not survive the flight, let alone the day. He lost a lot of blood. I've seen people die from less."

His eyes softened, like he wanted to ask her about what she had seen, but he held back and she was grateful that he did. Thinking about John was hard enough. She couldn't even imagine talking about him at that moment. She wasn't the type to cry and especially not in front of a handsome stranger with a badge.

"I have, too, but I'm optimistic for him because of you," he said, his voice supplicating.

She knew he was desperately trying to make her feel better and bring some solace to her, and though her emotions were still in turmoil, she decided to let him in. "Thank you, Ranger Hauser. Or is it 'Special Agent'?" she asked, glancing at his nameplate on his chest. She couldn't help but notice his well-defined pecs just under the surface of his brown shirt.

"Call me Pierce."

She gave a slight nod, but her cheeks warmed and she didn't know precisely why.

She would be lying if she said she hadn't noticed his muscular chest before, when he had been holding Anthony's body steady as it was lifted in the air by the helo crew. His arms were just as good. He worked out, but he wasn't entirely perfectly chiseled—he did have a little paunch that she would call one step away from a dad bod and admittedly made her even more attracted.

As she realized what she was thinking, right on the heels of John's memory, she snapped herself back to reality. She had no business thinking about the park ranger this way. He was a stranger who had been brought into her life by a tragedy; he would disappear in a few moments only to become a memory and a shadow in a story she would tell around campfires to come.

"I just wish there was something more I could do to help." She didn't know where her statement emanated from, but the moment it escaped her lips, she knew it was the truth. She felt so impotent standing there, not knowing if the man would live or die and likely never going to find out one way or the other.

Anthony had disappeared into the air and from her life. Beyond this moment in the woods, they had no other connections unless she continued to help—at least until they got word on his status.

"Is that your boyfriend over there?" he asked, motioning toward Matt.

She laughed aloud, almost snorting. "He's my best friend. His name is Matt. He's a bull rider and he is probably on the Garmin with his wife right now."

"Oh, glad to hear."

His last words fell flat and sat in the silence between them for a long awkward moment. "He was the one who really saved Anthony—if he makes it." She pulled at the back of her neck nervously. "Do you know what exactly attacked him?"

Pierce looked around like an animal was going to jump out of the woods at the mere mention of one. "I've been searching the ground for prints. Based on the wounds and the tracks I've found, I'm sure it was a mountain lion. Looks like just one. Probably a tom. They are looking for their own territories this time of year. Maybe he ran into it, but that is unlikely."

"So, what does that mean? Do you think the cat was stalking him?"

"I'm going to have to do some tracking to find out." He sighed. "And we'll have to find this cat. He needs to be taken care of."

"You're going to kill him?"

Pierce cringed. "I'd like to say no. If we can trap the cat and get him into a zoo somewhere, then maybe we can save him. Otherwise, his future may well hang in the balance. There are a few circumstances that could get the cat off the hook, though, if we could prove it wasn't really at fault—rather that it was human error that brought on the attack."

"*If* we find him or if we can prove the cat isn't at fault?"

Pierce put his hands up. "Wait... *We?*" he asked. "I can't

possibly take you with me while I'm tracking down a potentially dangerous animal which has already attacked one person and is more likely to attack another."

Matt stuffed the Garmin in his pocket and sauntered over toward them. "Sally is freaking out," he said, his words slow in true Matt fashion. He didn't seem to notice that he was interrupting, not even when Jamie shot him a look.

He wasn't always on top of things, but he had gotten more than his fair share of concussions while riding bulls. It was starting to show and was one of the reasons she had wanted him to join her in getting off the circuit for a while. He'd been great at the ranch for the last few months. Maybe she could even get Sally to come down, eventually.

"I'm sure she is," Jamie said. "She isn't going to like what we are about to do, either."

Ranger Hauser jerked as he looked over at her. "Don't you even think about it."

She waved him off. "You can let us help you willingly, or we can just follow behind you like little lost hikers. You pick."

He grumbled something under his breath. "You do know I have the power to arrest you, right?"

She smiled, knowing full well that she had won the battle. "You can't say you really want to be out in the woods alone with a rogue mountain lion on the loose. Besides, we can send Matt to the trailhead to let people know to turn around."

That elicited a smile, and it made him even more rakishly handsome. "There is a ranger on the way to close the trail, but it would be good to have Matt head down and herd tourists back who may have started up the trail."

"See, we are already proving invaluable." She sent him

her best smile and she wasn't sure, but she could have almost sworn that a red hue rose in his cheeks.

Matt looked over at Jamie and gave her a wink. "Just make sure my ass doesn't get chewed up by a mountain lion while I'm hiking alone, okay?"

She laughed. "You got it. Just call us when you get down to the trailhead. The good news is that you are probably going to run into tourists soon."

Matt nodded. "Fine, boss." He glanced over at Ranger Hauser. "Don't let her get hurt. She is good people."

Pierce smirked. "I have a feeling that when it comes to her and me, I'm the one who is in greater danger—and not from the mountain lion. This lady seems like hell on wheels."

Chapter Three

Pierce couldn't believe he had agreed to let Jamie tag along with him, and yet he had known without a doubt she was going to follow him one way or another. When it came to hardheaded women, he'd learned a long time ago that it was best to just let them do their thing. Some battles just weren't worth the fight.

If they came back without incident, he wouldn't even have to explain himself to his patrol captain. If push came to shove and Patrol Captain Reynolds met Jamie, he would see the futility he had faced as well.

He looked back at the blond woman and tried to control his smile. He'd be lying to himself if he tried to say he didn't like women like her. Sure, they drove him to distraction. His mother and sister were the same way, but they kept life interesting. If anything, they'd set him up to need women like them in his life—if a woman were a pushover, he wouldn't have known what to do with her.

"Did you see something?" she asked, looking at him and then down to the ground in fear.

As she did, he realized that as much as she was putting on a brave front in coming out here to help him hunt down a big cat, she was truly terrified. He couldn't blame her. For all they knew, the mountain lion had been watching them take care of Anthony the entire time. That was a lion's way—watching over their kill or returning to it to feed later.

There were studies that showed that in Yellowstone Park, the cats would have several caches and when wolves bothered them, they would lead them to one of the caches to get them off their trail. It worked wonderfully for the cats and the wolves got a free meal.

He had to admit, he didn't want to have a pack of wolves roll up on him and Jamie, either.

There was a break in the underbrush ahead of them and in the soft soil was a paw print. He pointed at it. "We are on the right trail."

She nodded, but she had a grim expression that made him wonder why she had wanted to come along with him. She could have left and gone back to her car with her buddy Matt and disappeared into the park never to be seen again. Yet she had chosen to remain—clearly, against her better judgment. She didn't want to be here.

He wanted to ask her outright, but he had a feeling that if he did, she wasn't about to give him a genuine answer. If she was staying to find the cat, that made her a bit of an adrenaline junkie—and while she'd said she and her friend were rodeo people, from the look on her face, the junkie angle didn't sit right. If she was staying to find out about Anthony, she could have just gotten Pierce's phone number, or he could have gotten hers. Then again, maybe she didn't want to give it out. Or, maybe, just maybe, she wanted to stay with him.

He chuckled at the thought.

If she didn't want to exchange numbers, she certainly hadn't stayed out here just to be around him. Besides, he wasn't that good-looking. At best, his sister had always told him he was a Costco four—cute, but not that cute.

Regardless of the reasons for her staying with him, Pierce was glad for the company. Usually, he was out here in the woods working by himself. If he were around people, they would be guests who would treat him like a tour guide and badger him with questions about the park. He spent his time reciting facts he'd been telling people over and over for the last seven years he'd been working there.

He enjoyed teaching, but he'd come here for the animals, they were far more manageable and usually better company—with Jamie being the one exception.

"How long have you been doing rodeo?"

"*Doing* rodeo?" she repeated, laughing and making him realize how ridiculous he sounded.

He looked back at her, opened his mouth and started to apologize, but before he could, she continued. "I barrel race on the circuit. I've been doing it since I was old enough to walk. My dad started me on the back of sheep in the local fairs and I've been going ever since."

"Is there a rodeo around here? I'd love to come to watch you. You must be good."

She walked past him, following the cat tracks as he slowed down. "I'm okay. I retired recently. Now I'm working for my brother's ranch, the West Glacier Cattle Ranch."

"I've heard of it."

She raised a brow as she glanced over her shoulder at him. "Oh?"

There were few from the area who hadn't after last summer's homicides. "I'm sorry for your losses."

"I appreciate that, but we weren't close." She studied him

and he gave her a look that spoke of his knowing of her father's misguided actions. "So, I'm sure you understand."

He could tell the subject made her uncomfortable by the way she sped up as she walked. He hurried to keep pace. "You wouldn't believe the number of deaths I deal with around here. There are far too many people who come here for things besides vacation, if you know what I mean." He changed the subject. "Sometimes I feel like I'm just a coroner. It seems like we always have people missing in the park. If I was smarter, I would have become a tour guide and taught people about bears or something."

She slowed down and waited for him to catch up. "You like animals?"

He shrugged. "They are better than the tourists. They don't really cause problems."

She pointed toward the direction they had come from where they had airlifted Anthony out. "Until they do."

"True." He nodded. "You can hardly blame them, since we are in their territory."

She glanced around, like she was suddenly aware of what they were doing and where they found themselves.

"Don't worry," he said, motioning toward the bear spray and gun on his utility belt on his hip. "You are safe with me. I deal with the wildlife in this park almost as much as the dead. In fact, they are the ones that usually tend to find the creatures first. They are the harbingers."

"What about the grizzly bears in the park? I always heard they were a major problem even with spray?"

"Besides wandering through the hotel or hiking trails, they really don't cause problems. They are predictable. They are looking for easy meals. As long as we keep the food and garbage locked up, they aren't too much of an issue."

"So, people become the easy meal?" she asked.

He pinched his lips but shrugged. "I hate to admit it, but pretty much. That, and when people leave coolers in the back of their trucks unattended."

She laughed. "You do realize that you just equated dead bodies as being the same as coolers."

"It's all the same to grizzly bears." He pointed to the ground. "And big cats."

She shook her head.

"Sorry," he said, "when you've been at this as long as I have, you forget that other people don't have the same jadedness. I forgot I'm not normal."

She smiled at him, shooting him an almost flirtatious look from under her lashes. "I'm good with abnormal."

Was it flirtation? No.

He couldn't have read her expression right. Not in the context of what they were talking about. She couldn't have been as warped as him. Most people didn't find the topic of dead bodies and predation a source for bonding. He had to be mistaken.

He moved past her as he tried to control himself and his overthinking. Clearly, he should have taken the week off, like Vince had told him. Maybe he shouldn't have gone back to work.

If he had told his ex-fiancée about the dead bodies, she would have flipped out. She hated that kind of talk. The only thing she'd ever wanted to talk about was the pretty things in the park, the flowers and the plants and the cool hiking trails that—oddly enough—she never actually wanted to hike.

In the end, Haven had left him. He hadn't been enough for her. When it came down to it, Pierce wasn't sure he was enough for any woman, and he wasn't sure he was ready to put his heart on the line again.

He paused for a moment, watching as Jamie moved up the game trail ahead of him. Her jeans hugged her curves, showing her strong hips. The muscles of her thighs pressed against the fabric, and he could see exactly why her horse must have responded to her touch. She was probably a dang good racer.

She stopped about a hundred yards up the trail, her face obscured by a large branch as she turned back to him. "Pierce!" She said his name with an edge of panic.

He rushed up the hillside. "What is it?"

"There's… I think you need to see this." She pointed to the side of the trail and a large patch of bushes.

He moved fast until he found himself at her side. She motioned to the game trail in front of them. There lay a piece of tattered and sun-bleached cotton fabric. At one point, he guessed the cloth might have been black but now it was a light gray striped with darker gray where it had been folded on the ground.

Bending down, he picked it up, expecting to stuff it in his back pocket to throw it away in his garbage bag in his pickup later. However, as he lifted the fabric, it unraveled and from within the decaying cotton a bony appendage rolled out and dropped onto the ground.

It took him a long moment to realize what he was looking at thanks to the drying and mummified flesh and blackened toenail—it was a human's big toe inside of what had once been a sock.

He dropped the sock onto the ground. He continued up

the trail toward Avalanche Lake and, not far off the main trail, lay a pair of men's hiking pants. They bulged in the area that would have been the right knee with what he assumed were bones. To the left and sticking out from beneath a wild azalea was a mandible, the teeth exposed with two large golden crowns on the back molars.

Beside the mandible was a human skull—or what was left of it, thanks to what appeared to be a gunshot wound on the left side of the man's head.

"Oh…" Jamie said, letting out a gasp.

"Don't touch anything," Pierce said, putting his hand up and stopping her from moving forward and disturbing anything further. "I'm not sure, but I think we found out why our mountain lion was around… He was still hungry after finding what looks like a possible homicide."

Chapter Four

Jamie had never been afraid of being alone, in the woods or of the dark, yet now that she was alone and standing in the dark and listening to the haunting sounds of an owl hooting in the distance, her skin prickled. A bird lifted from the pine limb beside her and made the branch crack, making her jump and cry out with surprise.

If Matt had seen her acting as she was, she would have been embarrassed. She glanced over toward the spotlights up on the hill where Pierce and his team had set up a makeshift crime scene around the remains while they waited for the coroner to arrive.

Another park ranger had arrived, someone he'd called Stephanie. She felt rather envious of the woman with her long brunette hair and even longer legs. The worst part of the woman was the penetrating gaze she had given Pierce when she had come to his aid. Anyone on the planet could have seen how much the woman cared about him. Heck, they could have felt it in the air—her desire was palpable.

They must have been together. If they weren't, Stephanie was definitely on the hunt.

Maybe she was the real cougar that Jamie needed to worry about—not that Stephanie had looked that old. In fact, and even more dishearteningly, Jamie had to guess she was at least a couple of years older than the woman. Even if she wasn't, she wasn't the type to tear down another woman for something outside of her control—if anything, with age came wisdom and really expensive Botox.

Jamie laughed at the thought.

If Pierce was the kind of guy to keep a stable of women, then she didn't need to think about him in the way she was thinking about him. Heck, as it was, she didn't need to be thinking about him. Period. He was nothing more than a park ranger passing in the night, literally.

They were simply two strangers meeting at a strange and macabre moment in time. A moment that was going to stick with her for the rest of her life but was likely nothing more than a Tuesday for him. This kind of thing, this level of stress and traumatic event, had probably made him like a crab in a pot of water: The trauma kept turning up the heat until the water boiled, and he was cooked.

She wondered if in some ways she had been the same way when it came to the rodeo circuit. It wasn't until John had died that she had realized she had grown accustomed to things no one else would have considered normal, or right.

Jamie feared the day she dealt with death with apathy. At least she still held hope.

The wind picked up and blew through the trees in the bowl of the mountain, making a whistling sound. It kicked up the waves on the lake and they crashed harder and harder against the rocky shoreline. The sound was cathartic, and it pulled her away from the thoughts of death, which surrounded her. In the moment, with the sparkling stars and unfaltering constellations, she was reminded of how insignificant she was in the world.

She walked to the edge of the lake and put her hand in

the icy water, opening and closing her fingers until her bones ached from the cold and she was forced to pull out. There was a smooth log on the well-trodden lake edge, and she sat down as she opened and closed her fist, trying to warm her chilled fingertips as she reveled in the pinpricking pain of her skin.

"Jamie?" Pierce's voice pulled her from her meditation, and she turned abruptly.

He was standing there with his arms crossed over his chest. "I'm sorry, I didn't mean to surprise you."

She moved to stand up, but he subtly waved for her to stay put and he sauntered toward her. The full moon illuminated his V-shaped body from behind and she tried not to stare. He was so handsome in the twilight, and she loved the way the shadows caressed the chiseled edges of his jaw. It made her want to trace the lines of the darkness until it swallowed them both.

"You look upset," he said, sitting down beside her on the log. His body pressed against hers and the warmth radiated through her, making her realize that even though it was summer, she was still cold. "Are you doing okay?"

She looked at his hand on his knees. Even they were beautiful with his sun-darkened skin and well-kept fingernails. There was a small bit of what appeared to be dirt under the nail of his pointer finger. As he noticed her staring at the tiny imperfection, he lifted the finger and pulled her from her inspection.

"I'm doing okay." And the only thing that was upsetting her was how badly she wanted to graze her fingers against him. "Have you gotten any word on how Lewis is doing?" She tried to pull the subject away from herself and back to the real reason she had stayed there.

"I haven't heard anything real recent, but that is usually a good thing." He glanced down at his watch. "I would guess he is either out of surgery or coming out of surgery soon. As soon as I hear anything, I promise I will tell you."

She nudged her knee playfully against his, the action almost out of place, and as she did, she felt the heat rise in her cheeks. She was glad it was dark and her face rested in the shadows.

Surprisingly, he didn't jerk away from her flirty touch. His reaction, or lack of one, made her question exactly how she felt.

"Did you find anything out about the body?" she asked, avoiding questions she didn't want to explore within herself.

He shook his head. "We found quite a number of bones, but no concrete source of identification for the remains."

"But do you have an idea of who they could belong to?"

He shrugged, and she didn't know how she should read his reaction but she knew enough that she should not continue to press.

"There are some missing folks in the area and some cold cases from throughout the years in the park I may have to look into," he continued, seemingly oblivious to her anxiety when it came to him.

"Do you think you can pull DNA?"

He nodded. "Sure, but that kind of thing is going to take a while. Often, we can get more information from our files and then put together enough pieces to get an identity and a probable cause of death long before we get answers back from the lab."

"Seriously?" she asked, shocked. She'd had no idea that tests took that long. "My cousin did an ancestry thing, and it only took a couple of weeks to get back."

"They aren't sending their samples in to a governmentally funded crime lab." He chuckled. "That being said, if we have a high-profile case that is getting a lot of media attention, we can usually get our tests put through quite a bit faster."

She nodded. "I'm not surprised."

"Yeah, it's amazing what a little negative press can cause."

Jamie opened her mouth and closed it as she thought about the blood on her hands and the implications it wrought.

He put his hand on her knee and looked her in the eyes. "Don't worry about it. This will all be fine." His voice was calm and as deep as she imagined his soul to be. "And, as far as Matt is concerned, he is in good hands as well. Neither of your names will be released to the press if you wish. However, I would like to honor you both with a citizen's merit award for springing into action in a moment of need."

Her blood pressure rose, thanks to his hand on her leg, and his words sounded as though they were being spoken from the other side of water.

"No."

His eyebrows quirked up. "Oh. Okay." He sounded a little hurt at her abruptness.

She put her hand on his as he tried to move his hand away. "No, not like that. Thank you for offering to give me an award, but I don't deserve anything. I just did what anyone would have done."

"What about Matt?"

"No. He wouldn't want something like that, either."

"You said he wasn't your boyfriend, but..." He glanced down at her ring finger.

"He's not, and I'm not married." She tried to control the heat rising within her. "My boyfriend was a bull rider and Matt's best friend. We all rode on the circuit together."

"So, you do have a boyfriend." He moved to pull his hand away, but she gripped him tighter.

"*Did.* He died." She spoke matter-of-factly. For the first time since he had passed, she didn't feel the lump in her throat when she said the words and she felt guilty at the lack of reaction.

She tried to tell herself it had been long enough that it was okay to have finally accepted that he was gone and she was ready to move on.

Pierce's fingers moved around hers and, as they did, she questioned if she was ready after all.

"I'm so sorry for your loss." He dropped his head. "I know what it's like to lose someone you thought you'd have in your life forever."

She and John had never promised forever of one another, but that was splitting hairs as they had certainly been together long enough to have gone the direction of marriage and children. "I'm sorry for yours," she said. "Do you want to tell me about it?"

He shook his head and pulled his hand away. "Not even a little." He stood up. "We need to start heading back. I'll get you back to your friend."

She'd never felt more rejected. Now she understood how he must have felt about her abruptness, and she questioned why she had ever chosen to stay behind.

Chapter Five

Pierce couldn't stop thinking about Jamie. She was like a ghost in the corners of his mind and, no matter how hard he tried to focus on his work, she kept popping up along the edges of his thoughts and pushing her way into the center of his attention. She was something else.

A few years ago, Vince had asked him about his ideal woman. They had been three sheets to the wind during their conversation, but he could remember telling his friend he didn't care what the woman looked like, but he wanted a woman who wasn't afraid to get her hands dirty—in fact, he wanted a woman who would walk in off the street and be unafraid to become a hero.

It hadn't been a street, rather it had been a trail, but Jamie was unquestionably a hero.

He thought of her admission about her deceased boyfriend. She had been quiet on the hike back to the parking lot. Under different circumstances, he would have loved to have made that hike with her up to Avalanche Lake—it was one of his favorites. Though it wasn't quite as good as a hike few tourists knew about and even fewer took thanks to the healthy population of grizzly bears and wolves in the area. The Hidden Lake Trail.

Since he had seen her drive away with her guy friend,

he had wished he had asked for her phone number. It would have been so easy, and he could have told her it was for any number of reasons, any of which would have seemed legitimate given the circumstances. Yet, his thoughts of where he should have been that week, and what he was supposed to be doing, had kept sprinting through his mind.

If only he had seized the chance to tell her the truth about himself and opened up, as she had. But he had never been the type to want to wear his heart on his sleeve. To do so was to risk being hurt again, and he had already been hurt enough for one lifetime.

He glanced over at the black-velvet box with Haven's engagement ring, which rested on top of the dresser his mother had given him as a child. Haven had hated everything in his house and especially the dresser—she'd said it was outdated thanks to its oak finish and brass handles—and, as soon as she'd moved out, he'd let the house sit almost empty except for his bed and that dresser for weeks.

It seemed somehow fitting that both things she had hated the most now sat together beside him. Though he was arguably the thing she now hated the most.

And that was exactly how he had fallen down the rabbit hole and missed his chance with Jamie—barbed memories of hate.

When Haven had left him, she had taken everything of value—including every shred of his heart. At least, he had believed so, until he'd seen Jamie on the mountain.

Between trying to control his staring and handling the mayhem he'd been presented with on the trail, he'd slipped into wondering if his attraction was lust or if it was driven by a more primal and dark force: the bloodied canine teeth of spite.

It was another of the many reasons he'd held back. It wasn't fair to Jamie or to him to flirt and shoot his shot when he was going after her for all the wrong reasons. If he started dating again, he didn't want to have Haven haunting his thoughts. That would be a major *if.* Dating sounded just about as fun as staring down a rabid grizzly bear on a narrow trail.

Actually, he'd rather run the odds on the grizzly bear.

He chuckled as he slipped on his utility belt and made sure it sat comfortably over his Kevlar vest and on his hips. It was bit of overkill to some to wear a bulletproof vest in the woods, but he'd learned a long time ago that it was best to prepare for the worst and hope for the best. And in this place, if it wasn't the environment or the animals that killed a person, there may be a person next in line who was happy and willing to do the job.

It was sad that nothing really surprised him anymore and he'd reached a point in life that death was just that... death. The end. Nothing more and nothing less.

There were things worse than death.

He knew.

He pulled his belt tight, so much so that it pinched his skin and reminded him of physical pain, taking away some of the edge of the emotional.

Since the loss of Haven, he'd sat on the edge of madness. He'd suffocated on the breakup. Wheezed around the memories of their laughter while he'd tried to fall asleep at night. He'd had to replace his pillow from smashing his fists into it too many times while trying to find comfort that he'd never seemed to find—until last night, when he'd finally found some solace in thoughts of Jamie.

He needed to see her again. Sometime.

As badly as he yearned to see her again, he wasn't under any misconceptions about attraction and lust. He knew exactly where it led—straight to heartbreak and loss, and he couldn't go through that kind of agony ever again. He was barely alive, even if he was breathing.

For now, he needed to focus on finding the mountain lion.

He checked his phone after locking his door and walked out to his work truck. Lewis was out of surgery and was in the rehab unit. He'd lost an eye, had received several units of blood and hundreds of stitches, but he was on the road to recovery. According to the nurse, he wasn't in a hurry to go hiking any time soon.

He couldn't blame the guy.

Big cats were one of the animals in this park that kept his head on a swivel. They were notorious for coming up from behind. Most people were afraid of the bears, but at least they were somewhat predictable, and a person could see them coming. This cat was going to come back to its cache, and it wasn't going to be happy about them removing the remains.

The good news was that it was likely to move on and disappear into the wilds once it found the body gone, but he would have to keep an eye on the trail for a few weeks to make sure visitors to the park were safe when traveling through the area.

He sighed as he found comfort in the predictability of his job. Maybe he would become one of those old rangers who lived in the single-room cabins, who went to bed at seven every night and got up at four every morning, and who focused their every waking hour on the constant barrage of blurring faces of tourists who came through the park's gates. They were as invisible to the tourists as the tourists were to them—just one more attraction for visitors to consume while on their vacation.

There was an ethereal beauty in their loneliness, and an element of altruism.

Yet, it was lonely nonetheless.

He wasn't sure he wanted to be lonely forever, or if it was fear that kept him tethered to his resolve to stick to promises of never dating until his memories of Haven dissipated.

In an effort to avoid the whirlpool of thoughts of loneliness and philosophy, he turned on the radio and tried to find solace in the guitar riffs of Tool. He tapped his fingers on the steering wheel as he navigated the empty road up to the Avalanche Lake trailhead. He'd slept far too few hours, but at least he'd slept more than the folks he'd tasked with holding the scene overnight. They would be glad to see the whites of his eyes this morning.

Stephanie was already at the trailhead when he arrived. She was smiling and her dark brunette hair was pulled into a tight French braid that landed halfway down her back. Most guys who worked at the park thought she was hot, and he couldn't deny she was pretty, but he didn't really care. She was good at her job and they got along great. Beyond that, everything else about her was just a benefit.

He pulled up to a stop beside her truck and rolled down his window. She walked over, flipped her braid over her shoulder and shot him a wide, almost too-warm smile. "Good morning, Pierce. You ready for a little of me in your life?"

He wasn't sure exactly what in the heck she meant by that statement, and he definitely wasn't sure how to respond without getting it all kinds of wrong.

"I'm ready for a hot cup of coffee and some good news, if that counts." He tried to avoid her verbal bullet.

"The good news is that you get me all day, if you want me. Second, we found more evidence this morning. We've already done the proper collection and cataloging. I have a bunch of pictures in my phone, if you want to take a look. We left everything in situ up there for you." She motioned in the direction of the back of her pickup.

"What did you find? Any further evidence as to the manner of death?"

"We found a speed loader for what looks to be a .45-caliber revolver."

"Did you find the gun?"

She shook her head. "No luck yet, but I called in a friend with dogs. Hoping maybe they can help us find exactly where the guy was killed and maybe there, we can pick up the gun."

He appreciated how she was on top of matters. "Send me a picture of the speed loader and its location in relation to the body. I don't need you today, you can go ahead and head home. I bet you're exhausted after being on scene all night." He tipped his head in appreciation and acknowledgment.

She glanced down at her watch. "Yeah, not gonna lie, I'm spent and the tourons will be showing up any minute now. They opened the gates thirty minutes ago. I'd rather not get stuck in a bear jam on my way back to my cabin. If you need anything…" She paused. "I'll be sleeping." She laughed.

"It will wait." He smiled. "Don't worry about a thing. As for the 'tourons,' they are called tourists. We've had meetings, don't let the captain hear you calling them that—

I don't want to have to sit in on another hour-long meeting about feelings."

"I'll stop calling them that when tourists stop acting like morons. Until that day, they are tourons in my book." She nodded, tapping the hood of his pickup with her hand in a goodbye. She smiled and waved as she turned away.

As she did, a white pickup pulled up on the other side of Stephanie's truck.

A blond woman in a cowboy hat turned to face him. *Jamie.*

His breath caught in his throat.

What was she doing here?

A broad smile lit his face, and he could feel it in his eyes. He tried to control himself and play it cool, but he couldn't control the tightening in his core.

Stephanie stepped over to his passenger's-side window and motioned for him to roll it down, her smile matching his. "I'll keep my ringer on. If you get done early, stop by. I'll have a pot of coffee on for you and a warm spot in my bed—if you're down." She spun on her heel and got into her truck before he even realized what she had implied.

He opened and closed his mouth, and his smile quaked into a look of shock. He had no idea what had just happened. Not really.

Stephanie was nice. He liked her. Most men would have given a foot and a couple of other body parts for what she had just offered him, but he wasn't interested in anything of the sort. He wasn't even sure if he wanted to think about another woman in bed yet.

As she backed up and pulled out, barely missing the front bumper of a rental car speeding down the road in the process, he found himself thinking of the ideas of feast or famine.

He stared down at his fingers on the steering wheel. There was a bit of dirt under the index finger on his right hand. He picked at it, wiping it free. It was stupid, he knew, but he normally got manicures. It was the one biweekly appointment he refused to give up. Tiffany would have his head if he came in with blood and gore under his nails.

Jamie tapped on his window and her facial features were tight.

He rolled down the window. He wasn't exactly sure what had happened to bring her back to this place this morning, but he was glad to see her. "Hi. Something I can do for you?"

"That's Stephanie, right?" She nudged her chin in the direction that Steph had just disappeared.

He nodded. "I thought I introduced you last night?" At the time, in the dark, he had thought nothing of it. Yet, last night he had introduced them together in a group of ten different responders and in the midst of conflict and elements of chaos. It was just a throwaway action that he hadn't thought about since. But now, in the light of day, there was some tension he hadn't expected, and he wasn't sure if it was coming from himself or the way Jamie had spoken her name.

"You did. I just didn't realize…" Her words tapered off like the thin flame of a freshly lit candle.

He wanted to tell her that there was nothing between him and Stephanie, but he wasn't sure if that was what she was talking about. If it wasn't, he certainly didn't want to bring it up. And, if it *was*, he didn't want to lie. Stephanie had come on to him, and regardless of the state of his feelings, he had never been one to deceive.

Chapter Six

How was it that when Jamie finally wanted to think about stepping back into the dating world, she picked a man who was inundated with women a thousand times prettier than her and gravitating in the man's circle? She wouldn't stand a chance.

Now, standing beside Pierce's pickup, she couldn't recall what she had been thinking this morning when she had woken up on the ranch and gotten in her truck and headed to the park. How could she think it was a good idea to come to this spot and try to reconnect with Pierce? It was only a shot in the dark that he would even be there again in the morning—she wasn't sure she was going to run into him again, let alone watch him carousing with a known threat of a woman.

She couldn't stand up to Stephanie, who was the perfect specimen of woman. Her breasts were perky and exactly the same size. Jamie's left one was slightly smaller than the right and when she looked in the mirror and flexed like she was throwing the lasso, the left lifted three inches higher. It looked almost grotesque. She couldn't even imagine what a man saw when she was on top and working away with him beneath. There her breasts would be, two little oranges moving around like marionettes on two independent puppeteers' strings.

It was a wonder anyone could even concentrate on the task at hand.

Perfect Stephanie probably didn't have the same issue.

She'd have perfect, well-placed tits. The kind that bounced like perfect little butter balls when she jogged and giggled with her gorgeous hair flouncing around her smiling face like she was an actress in some insipid commercial for minty fresh gum.

Ugh.

She really wanted to hate the woman. Yet she was enough of a feminist and proponent for other women to just be jealous and leave it there. Stephanie was probably as nice as she was *perfect*. Weren't they *always*?

There was something about the pretty ones with the ugly souls that somehow kept them from attaining true beauty. Then again, maybe it was her resentment of Stephanie that was assigning her with some benevolent *more*-ness.

She had to hope that her resentment was blind and, for once, it wasn't just love that cast the curtain of virtue.

Just because she wanted to like Stephanie didn't mean she was a good woman, just like all elders were not necessarily good people deserving of reverence and respect. Bad people came in all ages, genders, cultures and communities.

Only time would out.

That was, if she stuck around.

As she stared into Pierce's face, that was a topic of debate within herself. He was an incredibly handsome man, but she could look into his eyes and tell that he was lost. She couldn't explain exactly why, but there was a look within them that spoke of his being adrift in the sea of his thoughts and feelings. Feelings of what, she didn't know. However, she held out hope that there was a spark of desire for her.

"I'm surprised you're here. Did you lose something last night?" He ducked down and looked up the mountain toward the trailhead. "If you did, I can probably get you back up there to see if we can find it." He ran his hand over the back of his neck, nervously.

The only thing she had lost was her damned mind. Jamie couldn't tell him that she had only come back because she had wanted to talk to him again and that what had happened last night had kept her from getting any real sleep. She wasn't the kind of woman to let anything go half finished and apparently that extended to big cat attacks and dead bodies.

She tried to think fast. "I think I left my gloves up there, on the log where we were sitting. You know?"

"I don't remember you wearing any."

She felt her cheeks warm, but she had already started the lie and now she had to keep it going. "I... I took them off before you sat down. I think they fell off the log or something. I don't know. I was just going to run back up there if the trail was open and try to find them."

He nodded, appraising her features carefully, as though he were looking for something she wasn't saying. She glanced away before he could find his answer. "I'll go up with you. I need to check on my crew. The new investigation team is up there and looking for more evidence. I'm the lead investigator, so my boots need to be on the ground."

She nodded. "That sounds good. We can split up wherever you need. I don't want to be in your way." *I just want to get to know you more.*

Yet that wasn't the entire truth, either. Being that close

to the bleeding man had brought up so many memories about John. When she'd tried to sleep, images of her former boyfriend's face and the blood dripping from the corners of his mouth as he'd tried to speak had interwoven with the stranger's bloodied expression of fear as she'd tried to staunch the bleeding where the cat's teeth had penetrated his cheek.

She couldn't be alone, and she hadn't wanted to turn to Matt or anyone at the ranch. Matt had his own burdens to bear with John's death and she didn't want to appear any weaker than she already did when it came to her brother and their ranch hands—she had to appear strong. They were the Trappers, after all.

It was her and her remaining siblings jobs to repair the damage her father had wrought upon their name.

Pierce stepped out of his pickup.

Even though it was June, in Montana that still meant it was chilly in the mornings and she noticed he was wearing a thin coat over his uniform. Even through it, she could make out the V-shape of his torso that she could recall from his silhouette in the moonlight. He was built like a man who not only hiked but also lifted small trees and carried them around on his shoulders for fun in his free time.

Maybe he was the man behind the Brawny paper towel commercials. She giggled at the thought.

"Do I have something on my face?" he asked, running his hands over his chin self-consciously.

Though it was a tad bit evil, she dabbed at a spot by her mouth. "Yes, you have something. Right…there…" She reached over and touched his face where she had just been touching her own. There was a strange charge between

them, and she soaked it in like rays of the sun after a long,
dark winter.

His gaze drifted up from her fingers toward her eyes,
but she dropped her hand and turned away. "Got it." She
cleared her throat as if such an action could also straighten
up her feelings. "Let's go."

He grabbed something out of the back of his pickup and
slipped on a hiking pack as she walked over to her truck and
grabbed her own. Hers was filled with only a few essen-
tials: a knife, water, items to make a fire and bear spray in
an outside and reachable pocket. The last thing she wanted
to do was run into the cat who was probably still haunting the area.

She didn't know much about mountain lions, but she
couldn't imagine an animal like that going to the work of
attacking a human in an effort to protect its cache only to
run off—even if people were in the area. The Avalanche
Lake trail was always busy during the summer months.

There was a rental car parked in the lot and two older
hikers were putting on hats inside. She wanted to warn
them, but instead she simply pulled the straps on her pack
tighter. If Pierce didn't think they needed to close the trail,
she had to trust his judgment. The last thing she would want
was some stranger coming up to her and freaking her out if
she was about to go into the woods on a long hike that made
her halfway nervous as it was, thanks to the many signs and
brochures already warning about the animals in the area.

Yes, it wasn't as if they hadn't already been told.

She looked over at Pierce, who had started to head toward the trail. Hurrying, she caught up, her pack shuf-
fling and making a rubbing sound on her polyester coat
as she moved.

For the first half mile, they moved quickly, and he loudly hummed a song she didn't recognize. The second time he started the same song, she realized it was just something he did so that they didn't surprise animals along the trails, and she appreciated the simple action. She'd heard about people wearing bells along the trails, but in her family, they had always been a joke—simply called dinner bells.

Now, after last night, she kind of wished she was wearing one. Though she wasn't sure they would work on a big cat or if the noise would only let the cat know exactly where to find them.

She was freaking herself out and she moved in closer toward Pierce, who was leading the way. As she did, he once again looked back at her, checking to make sure she was safe. He smiled as he hummed. "You are doing great. How's the pace for you?"

"Good." She motioned toward the wooden pathway. "Flat is easy. It's when we start gaining elevation that it gets fun."

His smile widened and he moved so she could hike beside him in the widening trail. "I've done some backcountry hiking in this park where we gain a thousand feet elevation in less than a half mile. It gets wild. You have to use trekking poles and lines."

"I'm one for a good adventure, but that is not my kind of hiking. In fact, I wouldn't even call that hiking anymore—that is straight mountaineering. That's impressive."

"What's impressive were the women who were doing it in the 1800s in those huge skirts." He motioned around his legs like he was wearing a Victorian skirt. "There are pictures of women wearing them on the tops of the mountains after having hiked up in them and high-heeled shoes."

"How would they see where they were stepping?" she

asked, imagining the logistics of the women who had undertaken such feats.

He shrugged. "You would know more about that than I would."

She thought she was tough, running headstrong horses at high speed. Yet, she wasn't sure she had anything on women who were willing to blindly stride up treacherous, nearly vertical mountainsides in a time in which women were expected to do little more in high society than be window decorations in their husband's affairs.

As they moved up the mountain, he showed her flowers—a yellow glacier lily that had just popped up and come into bloom and a three-petaled white flower called a trillium near a small spring. He pointed out dozens of mushrooms and plants and she found solace in his voice and passion for nature. He was so handsome as he spoke about what he loved as he hiked up the mountain toward their destination, she could tell why he had chosen to become a ranger—the job fit him.

He moved *with* the swollen, exposed roots and tearing, jagged rocks like they weren't problems to be overcome but opportunities to stretch and move his body. He flourished in the journey and the experience that nature provided.

She hadn't noticed it last night, but it made sense given everything that had been taking place.

Pierce bent down, his backpack shifting slightly as he motioned toward a small, needled bush on the side of the trail. "This is a yew bush," he said, smiling back at her. "It was used by Native Americans in their healing ceremonies. Modern pharmaceutical companies ended up studying it, and using the compounds found in it to make cancer-fighting drugs."

She loved how smart he was and, as he let go of the plant and it bobbed beside his leg as he stood up, she stared at his round, muscular thighs. He was even more handsome with every passing second. There wasn't a thing about him that wasn't *perfect*.

He was so out of her league. All she had going for her was an infamous family name and a ranch in disrepair while he had the world endlessly at his fingertips.

Continuing, they moved up the trail and Jamie could tell from the length of his steps that he was slowing down to make sure she was able to keep up with him. They stepped off the trail where she had helped Anthony. She had expected to see blood staining the ground where he had lain, but aside from a small patch on a yellowed, decaying leaf and upturned dirt, there was little to indicate the chaos that had taken place—even the coffin-shaped impression had disappeared over night.

In the distance, she could start to make out the sounds of the team working on the recovery of the remains and as they rounded a corner, a man in a red coat came into view. As the man looked up and noticed them, he gave them a two-fingered wave.

"That's David Slayton. He is a member of our Avalanche and Search and Rescue Teams as well."

She nodded, waving back at the good-looking and thin man waving down at them from up on the mountain.

"He and Stephanie used to be an item."

The hair on the back of her neck raised slightly. "Is that right?" She didn't want to be annoyed at the mere mention of the woman's name, but she couldn't help herself. "What happened there?"

He shrugged. "She has a tendency to jump around between men. It's one of the many reasons I would never date her."

It was like he was making a point of reassuring her, but she wasn't exactly sure why unless he was feeling the same pull and attraction that she was feeling toward him.

For the first time since she had seen him this morning, she felt as though she really had a chance at something more than just a simple friendship. While she wasn't exactly sure what she wanted from Pierce, she was grateful to be close to him and back in his circle and away from the ranch. For at least the next few hours, she could escape from the memories of the past that always seemed to sweep her up and carry her away to the gaping maw of endless pain.

Chapter Seven

David walked down the game trail and met them halfway. He had an excited expression on his face, and he stopped sideways on the trail, motioning for Pierce to follow. "Good morning, Special Agent Hauser." He dipped his head toward Jamie. "Ms. Trapper. Glad to see you back today." He shot Pierce a questioning look.

"Morning," Pierce said. "We touched base with Stephanie at the trailhead. She said you found a speed loader. Anything else of note? Any more sign of the cat?"

"We haven't seen the cat. I have a call out to the K-9 unit out of Kalispell. They will be here any time. They aren't used for treeing cats, but we can get a team for that if you want to mitigate the problem."

Pierce shook his head. "Nah. The cat was just doing what a cat naturally does, I don't think it is going to continue posing problems if it hasn't attacked anyone else. I'm expecting with us working here for a few more days, we may push it out. Let's see how this goes."

David nodded. "Didn't you hear? Patrol Captain Reynolds called before you arrived. He wants us to be out of here by the end of the day."

"What? You have to be kidding me. That makes absolutely no sense. With the dogs coming in? We haven't even finished collecting evidence. He must have lost his mind."

"He said he was worried about the missing hiker in Spring Valley." David shrugged and motioned vaguely in the direction of that area.

The hiker had been missing for a year and they had long ago given up looking for the man's remains, so it made no sense that when they had an active case his boss would suddenly want to focus on a cold case.

"Why would he be worried about that guy?"

David shrugged. "I think he said something about the fact that we have enough to ID this vic and anything else was just sugar on top."

Clearly, his boss needed to retire if he didn't actually want to do an investigation. They were law enforcement officials. Sure, they didn't work in Chicago or New York City, but that didn't mean that causes of deaths didn't need to be solved. Just because this case was a little more challenging than normal and would require a greater degree of effort, time and money didn't mean that they shouldn't pull out the stops. Just identifying the individual was hardly enough.

He opened his mouth to speak but he bit his tongue. Speaking his mind and sharing his concerns with David and Jamie wasn't appropriate. They didn't need to know or hear about interoffice politics or what could possibly turn into infighting. He was a professional. When he got a chance to speak with the patrol captain, Eliot Reynolds, he would clarify a few things—and make sure what he was hearing was accurate before jumping to conclusions. There was no sense sending his blood pressure out of control over what could possibly be a poorly translated conversation.

"If you don't mind, David, I'm going to go ahead and give the patrol captain a call."

David nodded. "That's probably a great idea. In the meantime, I'll make sure the night crew finishes up our paperwork and then morning crew is briefed for the day."

He gave the man an appreciative nod as he dialed Eliot's number. Jamie was leaning against a tree not far from him down the narrow trail. She was looking into the distance, pensively. She was probably thinking about how inept this investigation was. At least, she would be if she had ever been around any kind of investigation before. He hoped not. That way she didn't have any kind of barometer, and there was a chance he'd still appear somewhat in control and maybe even a little bit cool.

His call went to voicemail, and he hung up. He'd call him back later.

Jamie walked over, and she brushed her hand against his lower back as she carefully stepped around him on the narrow trail. "If your boss is on you about the time, then we need to get to work."

David looked at him with a quirk of the brow, questioning if they were really going to allow her to participate in the search. It wasn't conventional, but if the patrol captain was breathing down their necks and really wasn't interested in anything besides identifying their victim and not looking at this death at anything besides a suicide, then they were no longer dealing with a potential crime scene.

Whether he agreed or not, thanks to his boss wanting to sweep this death under the rug, the rules had now effectively changed.

Jamie walked up the trail and broke off up to the right and into the woods. "Wait!" he called after her.

She stopped.

David could think what he wanted. They wouldn't be on this mountain if it hadn't been for Jamie—she was the one who had found the hiker and saved his life, and then she had also found the remains. If anything, she had proven her merit and deserved to be here. In the future, if she was interested, he would have to talk to her about joining the volunteer search and rescue team he was involved with in Flathead County. She would be a perfect addition to the unit.

He hurried toward her. "Do you have bear spray?"

She nodded and pointed at the can in her pack.

"Perfect. If you're out here by yourself, I want you protected. Just make sure you're upwind if you use the spray, or you will be as incapacitated as the animal you're trying to stop."

"I can't say that I really want to be out here by myself," she said, her voice barely above a whisper. "I mean, I can... I'd just rather have you with me." She glanced over at David.

Her candor surprised him. *Was she trying to rescue him?*

He couldn't help the smile that graced his lips. "You don't have to. I need still get a hold of the patrol captain and get some answers, but I have a feeling that I'm going to get answers I don't want."

She nodded. "In situations like that, I have found it can be better to feign ignorance. If a problem arises with your boss, just blame it on me. Tell him I was pushy or something. It's easier to ask for forgiveness—and I don't mind being your fall guy."

He laughed. "I'm not that kind of person, but I appreciate your willingness to fall on the sword. There're other work-arounds to this, though."

She chewed on the corner of her lip like she was thinking. "Do you guys ever work with local cops?"

He nodded. "Sometimes, if things require extra hands, we call in locals to create a joint task force."

She had a mischievous look on her face and her eyes sparkled. "My brother just got married to a detective. Her name is Emily Monahan. She could help—this is right up her alley. She's great."

"I like your thinking." It was a great idea, but he didn't know how he was going to make it happen. Under normal circumstances, he would have to get Reynolds's sign-off on a task force. "I'm just hoping we can find something today that makes it impossible for Reynolds to take us off this. Or, enough that if he gets his way, we can find the answers we need to pull together the events that led to this person's death—even if it was accidental or something else. This person's family deserves answers."

They searched in silence. The sound of the creek grew quieter as he moved farther up the mountain and away from the initial area they had found the person's jaw. They dropped over the top of the ridge and into the next ravine. The brush grew thick and clawing. Even if there were ten bodies in here, the only way they would find them is if they fell on the top of their hiking boots.

"Jamie?" he called to her.

"Yeah?"

"Let's start working our way back." He stepped out of the bushes. As he did, he saw the eyes. The big, black, cat eyes.

The mountain lion crouched low to the ground as it stalked him.

He grabbed his Glock, unholstering it.

He didn't want to shoot the cat.

"Hey!" he yelled, pointing the gun at the mountain lion's chest. "Hey, cat! Get back!" He lunged toward the animal without thinking.

The animal jumped up, and spun on its feet. The cat's tail whipped as it turned and started to run in the other direction. The lion turned and looked back at him one more time until it disappeared into a thicket of bushes.

Jamie moved behind him. "Is it gone?"

He nodded. "Stay close."

She was holding the bear spray in front of her body. Her hands were shaking, hard.

He slipped his gun back in its holster, putting his hand on his belt in an effort to control his own. He didn't want to let her see that he, too, was scared.

He motioned to the canister. "It's going to be okay. The cat won't be back. They are pretty skittish." She lowered the can to her side. Reaching over, he took hold of her free hand. "You're okay."

She nodded, but he could feel how tense she was, and he could understand her fear.

He held her hand as he walked with her to a small opening. "Here," he said, motioning for her to sit down. "Let's take a second. Regroup."

She didn't say a word as she allowed him to help her to sit. He reluctantly let go of her hand as she settled onto the ground. He sat down beside her, hugging his knees to his chest.

He scanned the area around them for the beady eyes of the animal that had been stalking them. He had only been half telling the truth. There was no way to know if the cat had left or not. It could have still been watching, for all he knew, but he wasn't about to tell her that the mountain lion could have still been on the hunt.

For now, all he could do was try to control the narrative and help her believe that they were going to be okay.

She was staring in the distance the cat had disappeared.

"You okay?" he asked.

She didn't move for a long moment, but finally she turned to look at him. "That cat was even bigger than I remembered. I can't believe Anthony survived. He fought so hard."

Reaching down, his fingers brushed against something hard that, at first, he thought was a rock. But as he ran his finger over the surface of the object, he realized it was pitted. Looking down to where his hand rested. He pulled his arm back.

Where his fingers had been lay a rib bone.

He stood up.

It was undeniably a human rib, as it was sharply curved and narrow. It had chew marks on it from where an animal, likely of the rodent kind, had feasted.

Not far to his left lay a tattered leather wallet. He reached down and picked it up. Inside was a man's driver's license. He recognized the face and the name: Clyde Donovan.

"Wow." He let out a long exhale.

He had thought getting stalked by the mountain lion was going to be the most dramatic thing to happen to him today. He was wrong. This was going to cause problems.

"Whose wallet is it? Do you recognize them?" she asked, sounding concerned.

"Yes…yes, I do. It's the mayor who went missing over a year ago. A man who had his fair share of enemies."

Chapter Eight

The ranger headquarters was situated in a dark brown log cabin set behind a café and shop in the small town of Apgar just inside the gates of Glacier. Jamie had driven by the place dozens of times throughout the years and had never noticed its presence, let alone realized its function.

A woman was typing away in the far corner, not bothering to look up as they walked in. She had headphones on and seemed hyperfocused on whatever it was she was working on. Aside from her, it appeared as though no one else was there. For this late in the evening, it made sense.

There were a few dozen desks, most empty aside from stacks of papers and files waiting to be handled. A few had pictures of families, one playing football in matching red-and-blue uniforms. Her family wouldn't have been caught dead doing anything of the sort, but it made her smile.

When her father had been alive, they had all been expected to help out around the ranch. There were always jobs to do. She'd been in charge of the barn and the horses. She had cleaned more stables and dragged more pastures than she cared to think about. Yet, that was how she had fallen in love with horses and had turned that love into barrel racing. She was always outside with her horses.

Her favorite horse growing up had been a well-bred Appaloosa named Fancy Face. The horse had been hers since before she had even started to walk. In fact, before her death, her mother had taken pictures of Jamie in a diaper riding on the back of Fancy Face. There was some discussion that her first real words were the horse's name.

She'd had her until her senior year of high school. One day she had come out and Fancy had passed. There had been no warning, and it had been quick, but the hole her passing had left in Jamie's life had been almost as immense and impossible to fill as the loss of her mother.

"A penny for your thoughts?" Pierce asked, giving her a pensive look.

A thousand dollars wouldn't buy them from her at the moment. "Oh, I was just noticing the pictures around your office. And I'm surprised this is all the rangers that work at the park." She motioned around the room. In total, there had to be no more than twenty-five desks and an office at the end of the room with a door that read "Patrol Captain Reynolds" on the glass.

He looked around as if he suddenly noticed how small the room really was. "Oh, yeah." He sighed. "There are a variety of different types of park rangers within Glacier and all federally owned parks. This office is just for the law enforcement side of things here. We don't have many on staff. The Feds don't like to give us too much money."

She was a long way from shocked. "Do you think that your captain will still want to you to back off this case now that we have a possible ID?"

He shrugged. "I couldn't believe he wanted me to in the first place." He spoke in barely a whisper as he glanced toward the man's office. "I've worked with him a long time. This is a first."

The subject made him uncomfortable, but she couldn't understand the captain's thinking at all. She pulled out her phone. Her fingers trembled as she looked at her contacts list and she considered texting her sister-in-law, Detective Emily Monahan, and telling her who and what they had found in proximity to the person's remains.

Emily would sink her teeth into this man's death and run. The investigation would be so different in her hands. Yet, perhaps Jamie was jumping the gun.

She pushed her phone back into her pocket. "Let's see how this meeting goes. He does know I'm coming with you, doesn't he? I don't want it to be a surprise."

He nodded. "I told him you made the discovery. He wanted to ask you some questions."

"I don't know what I could possibly help him with." She thought about Emily again. She always talked about suspects and people she brought in for questioning when she was investigating crimes. One of her favorite idioms was "A fish that keeps its mouth shut rarely gets hooked."

For some reason, it felt important in this moment.

"He can be a little intimidating, but don't fall for his façade. He is actually a pretty nice guy—most of the time."

She didn't want to point out that ever since she'd met Pierce, his boss had seemed far from nice—if anything, he seemed to be running on the fine line between honorable and wrong. In fact, she could even argue whether the way he was acting was legal or ethical.

"I'll try to trust your judgment."

He sent her a crooked half grin. "I have been wrong when it comes to people before, so feel free to use your own. I'll have to tell you about what I was supposed to be doing this week sometime." There was an edge of pain in his voice that made her want to ask him right now. But before she could ask, he turned away and strode toward his commander's door.

The knock reverberated through the nearly empty space. Finally, the woman in the corner looked up and seemed to notice them. She had a long scar over the bridge of her nose.

Though Jamie wasn't entirely sure, she could have sworn she smelled the sharp odor of fear in the air.

The woman started to open her mouth but slammed her lips shut and then stared back at her computer. Pierce didn't seem to notice as he tapped his knuckles on the glass of Reynolds' door.

"Come in." The man's voice was thin and raspy, like that of someone who'd smoked most of his life and lived in the bar for the remainder. Or maybe he just struggled to breathe.

She followed Pierce inside, keeping her gaze on the floor until he motioned for her to take the seat to the right while he took the gray cloth chair to the left.

Jamie sat down. In front of her was a man in a large black wheelchair. The device had all-terrain wheels. He had a joystick to control direction, and as she looked at him, Reynolds gave her a wave. "Good afternoon."

She tried to not act surprised. Pierce hadn't mentioned the man used a mobility aid.

"Nice to meet you…" She paused, unsure of exactly how to address the man. She glanced at Pierce for guidance.

Before he could speak, the captain spoke. "You can call me Eliot."

And just like that, she felt like a jerk for thinking ill of him.

"Nice to meet you, Eliot. I'm Jamie Trapper."

Eliot tipped his head. "So I've heard. Your reputation as a lifesaver precedes you. Thank you for the work you did in helping the man on the trail. I hear he is recovering well from the attack."

"I did what I thought was right." Her thoughts moved to this morning and how close they had come to becoming victims of attacks themselves. "Did Pierce tell you about our run-in with the mountain lion today?"

Eliot's gaze moved to Pierce. "What is she talking about?"

He nodded. "With the new findings, I forgot to tell you we had a minor bluff charge. The cat took off. I think the animal is just trying to protect its food caches, nothing more."

"Did it look unhealthy?" Eliot asked. "Do you think there is something we need to be concerned about as far as guests are concerned?"

"I keep saying I don't think so, but I've just been proven wrong," Pierce conceded. "I hate to make promises or assurances about things I can't guarantee. If anything, the only thing I can say with any degree of certainty is that if there are other bodies out there, or other caches that this animal has and a hiker crosses its path—this animal will attack."

A stone dropped in her stomach, but she didn't know exactly why. Perhaps it was the fact she hadn't even considered that there would be more dead bodies out there. In fact, there was nothing to say that the rib and the wallet weren't from a second body that had nothing to do with the remains she had initially located.

In fact, they could be dealing with a serial killer.

She was glad she was seated as her knees weakened at the thought.

If there was a serial killer dropping bodies in the park, and if they were watching the news of them locating the remains, did that mean she and Pierce would be placed in the sights of the killer? They could very well become the next targets. If they were taken out of the picture, they couldn't testify about their findings in a court of law. It would weaken any case a prosecutor would have—certainly not make or break it, but if a person was desperate to keep themselves from going to prison…

The thought made the hair rise on her arms.

It was true; no good deed went unpunished.

No, she was getting ahead of herself.

Eliot pulled something up on his computer screen. "We have been making headlines—already. This is what I was afraid of. In light of the new findings, I think it's important that we keep the cat under control and this new charge under wraps. Fair?"

It seemed wrong that he was asking them to hide the fact there was a dangerous animal on the loose but, given that there may have been a far more dangerous human out there, helped to keep her concern in proportion.

"What do you want to make of the mayor?" Pierce asked, his voice taking on a steely edge.

Something about Eliot shifted and he grew nervous, his gaze moved quickly around the room. "I hate this is in our laps."

"I think we should call in the locals—get a task force together. Detective Emily Monahan is Jamie's sister-in-law."

Eliot's face paled and he opened his mouth to speak but he closed it and took a moment before starting again. "I was hoping we could get away from this entire incident. It looks like that is going to be an impossibility."

"Is that why you told David you wanted us to work on the other missing person case?"

Eliot answered with a tiny nod. "So much for wishful thinking. There will be no minimizing this. As such, I need you to get going. Call in the task force. We have an ID. I had David run the remains to the state crime lab in Missoula. They are expediting their tests. I'm hoping we can at least find out if we have two victims or one within the next couple of days."

"Did you notify the mayor's family of the findings?"

"Don't worry about that until we have absolutely no doubt it's him. We don't want to make mistakes, given his family ties." Eliot gave Pierce a sharp look. "For now, you just handle pulling together the team. Vince can help when he comes back from vacation tomorrow. You guys need to find the gun. And, if this was a homicide, we need to find out who pulled the trigger."

Chapter Nine

Jamie was quiet as they walked out of headquarters and to his pickup.

"Want to go with me?" Pierce asked, looking over at Jamie.

Her face was tight and there was a look of hurt and confusion in her eyes. "That's fine. We can leave my pickup here."

It had been a strange meeting with his boss, but at least he had finally gotten somewhere with the man and received the approvals he'd wanted and needed to move forward. Yet, it still sat foul with him that Reynolds would have wanted to pull him off the death if they hadn't found the possible identity of the man—and learned it was the missing mayor.

And why hadn't he wanted him to do the death notification? Usually that fell to the highest-ranking officer, which was Pierce, to tell the family of the victim. He didn't see Reynolds handling it himself, he wasn't the type. That meant he must have been handing it off to David or someone else. Or, maybe he was just waiting until they had absolute confirmation on the ID.

If that was the case, he could understand. He wouldn't want to cause the family undue grief and heartbreak only to later learn that the remains they had located were, in fact, not Clyde's.

Yet he hadn't been wanting to give the notification in that moment.

He walked to the passenger side of the pickup and opened the door for Jamie. He waited for her to step up inside before closing the door and making the way over to his seat and getting inside. She turned to him as he clicked his seat belt into place, "What aren't you telling me about yourself?"

He was taken aback by her abruptness. "What? What do you mean? Are you upset with me?"

She shook her head. "I'm not mad." She softened her tone but he could tell she was forcing herself to remain calm. "Why would Eliot treat you with kid gloves? It was like he was worried about your feelings. Is there something going on with you that you aren't telling me? You said something earlier…"

For the first time today, he wished he was back dealing with the dead. "Are you hungry?"

"Are you just trying to avoid my question?" The anger returned to her voice.

He reached over and put his hand over hers, hoping she wouldn't pull away. When she didn't, he sent her a soft smile. "I promise I *will* tell you everything. I just need a minute."

She let out a long exhale and it made him want to tell her everything about Haven now. He looked at his watch and, as he did, he realized exactly what day it was, and his heart sank.

He needed the minute more than ever.

"I'll cook. I have steaks at my place. You okay with that?

I'm a pretty good cook. When we are done, I can bring you back and you can grab your pickup, or whatever you'd like. I'm sure you want to get back to it."

She nodded but remained quiet.

He hadn't meant to hurt her feelings or make her shut down. If anything, he'd wanted things to go in exactly the opposite direction. She was an incredible woman, and he had enjoyed every second he had spent with her—which was strange, given what they had been doing together.

It didn't take long for them to leave the gates of the park. He lived outside the park, near Hungry Horse Reservoir, with a place right along the edge of the lake. His mother and father had left him the house when they had passed away. When Haven had been living with him, she had taken most of his parents' things out and put them in the garage, replacing them with kitschy knickknacks and *Live Laugh Love* signs throughout the place.

When she'd moved out, she'd taken everything with her that was even remotely tied to her. Instead of buying anything new, with the exception of a 65-inch television from Costco, he'd gone out to the garage, pulled in all of his parents' old furnishings and put them back in the house. The pièce de résistance was his parents' old green-velvet couch complete with dark green fleur-de-lis that had been handed down from his mother's parents.

It was like stepping back in time, and it even carried the faint smell of his childhood. He couldn't quite put his finger on the scent, but if forced to explain, he would have said it was fryer grease mixed with his father's aftershave and his mother's at-home perm kits.

His thoughts moved to Jamie's family. All he really knew about the Trappers was what had been in the local newspaper, and he knew well enough to realize only half of what he read was true—and sometimes not even that much when it came to them making sure they had a good story. The truth was often obscured by perspective and battle lines.

"How many siblings do you have? You said your brother was married to Emily— What is his name?"

She looked surprised that he had suddenly broken the silence between them. He shouldn't have brought up her family when he was avoiding his own past, but maybe it would make it easier for him to explain things and not come off soft or like some loser.

He could tell she wasn't the kind of woman who wanted a guy in her life who was a pushover. She had dated a bull rider and her best friend was a bull rider. Her family was a ranching family. She could control a thousand-pound horse with her thighs. There was no way she would want a man like him in her life if he told her the truth.

"I had two brothers. My oldest brother died, I'm sure you heard about it, with my father. For a long time, the local police thought it was a murder-suicide. It was a whole thing. My other brother, Cameron, runs the ranch now. And then I have a sister who is younger than I am, who is running around Hollywood somewhere. Last time I saw her, she was in a commercial for yogurt." She laughed. "That was actually kind of cool."

"Do you talk to her?"

She shook her head. "I'm not even sure she knows my father's gone. And even if she did, I don't think she would care. My father was the epitome of misogyny. If I hadn't left home, I'm pretty sure he would have tried to have sold me off to the highest bidder to get me married and out of his hair."

He'd known her father'd had a reputation as a piece of work, but he'd not known the degree to which she'd suffered. Some of her hardness and also her capability and adaptability made sense. "It's no wonder you're so strong. I'm sorry you've had to go through everything you've had to go through."

She closed her eyes as she ran her fingertips over her temple. "I wish I would have gone to college. I always did well in school. However, that really wasn't an option for me. My father refused to help me with financial aid, and I couldn't afford to do it on my own even with some of the scholarships I received. I think that was the moment I really decided that I was going to leave the ranch and never come back."

And yet here she was. He couldn't imagine everything she was feeling in having returned to the one place she'd sworn she would never return. The more he learned about her, the more he wanted to take her in his arms and rescue her. However, he wasn't sure that that was what she was looking for; if anything, it seemed as though she was looking to find answers about herself.

"There's a pretty good community college here in Kalispell. What would you go back to school for?" he asked.

"I love animals, so I spent a lot of time thinking about veterinary medicine. However, after John's accident and now this, I don't know if I want to deal with trauma."

The rawness of her statement made him hurt for her. He could certainly understand her feelings. "I know how hard it is to compartmentalize."

"Compartmentalizing is what got me to where I am today."

Road noise sat between them like static on an old television, heavy and tense.

Maybe he wasn't as soft as he thought he was. Or maybe he had gotten her wrong. Perhaps, she was softer than he realized.

His old cabin sat at the end of the gravel road, tucked back in the timber. Hungry Horse Reservoir sat at the edge of his property, and he had a long dock that stretched out into the lake. As they drove up and parked, a white-tailed buck that was grazing on a bush near the cabin's front window lifted his head. He switched his tail, annoyed that they would interrupt his feeding.

"That's Gregory Peck. He was born on the property about six years ago. The doe who had him had lived here for ten years before that." He smiled at the thought. "It's funny how you get connected to the animals, even the wild ones. My parents had named the doe Fauna. She was around for a long time. My mom really enjoyed watching her. Some years she'd even have twins."

"My mom was like that on the ranch, too. We had a herd of elk that would always come down from the mountains during the fall. There was one cow that my mom had rescued when it was a calf and got stuck in our fence. After that, this elk would always come up to the front door in the mornings and bed down while my mom had her morning coffee."

He could tell from the tone in her voice that she missed her mom just as much as he missed his own. It amazed him that they had both been through so much loss and yet they were both relatively young. It made him wonder how much more life would deal him—good and bad. It also made him wonder how much a single person could withstand before they lost themselves.

"Gregory Peck probably won't run when we go to the front door, just so you know. However, he doesn't know you, so he may, so don't be alarmed."

Some of the heaviness that had seemed to weigh on her dissipated as she opened the truck door and stepped out. The deer switched his tail again, but didn't bother to move. He looked at Jamie and then at Pierce, and then the deer put his head back down and started grazing on the bush once again.

Gregory Peck was the closest thing Pierce had to a dog, so he was glad that he had his deer's approval. It was silly, but he took it as a sign. Deer were extremely skittish creatures, and if he didn't feel the need to run from Jamie then Pierce could definitely tell her his truth without fear that she would turn against him.

They moved quietly inside and Pierce closed the door behind them.

"So, his name is Gregory Peck. Does that mean that you are a fan of classic movies?"

"Yes, *To Kill a Mockingbird* is one of my favorites and his best role." He smiled. "I'm a huge fan of classic movies and books. I'm a big reader. Around here, as I'm sure you know, technology is an amenity sometimes and electricity can be hit or miss in the winter. Books are always available and there's nothing better than sitting in front of a wood-burning stove and reading at night before you go to bed."

She tilted her head as she looked at him, appraisingly, and he was struck by how beautiful she truly was, inside and out. Those eyes had a way of just stopping him in his tracks. "You have got to be kidding. I used to get made fun of all the time on the rodeo circuit because I was the big nerd who would sit at the trailers and read while everybody else went to the bars and wanted to get rowdy."

"You can't tell me you didn't get rowdy once in a while. I thought we weren't lying to one another." He laughed, the sound coming from his core, and it felt good. It was the kind of laugh that he hadn't experienced in a long time, and he hadn't realized how much he had missed it until now.

Her eyes sparkled. It was stupid that he noticed such a thing, but they really did. Maybe it was the light, or maybe it was their being with one another, but it was like something in the way she looked at him had awakened.

Or maybe that was wishful thinking.

"Oh, I can be rowdy. You know what they say about barrel racers..."

"What is that?"

"It's always said in rodeo that the barrel racers are the wildest bunch out there. There's nothing we won't do— and I can honestly say that that's normally true. Some of the girls I raced with were balls-to-the-wall, all the time. They were a lot of fun, but you can only keep up that level of energy for so long."

"If you could, would you want to go back to rodeoing again?" he asked, careful not to bring up the accident and any pain it may cause.

She shook her head. "I tried to stick with it, I did. I just got...*old*."

"You're far from old." He led her toward the kitchen as they spoke.

"Old doesn't have anything to do with age—not there, and not even in life. You know?"

He did. He knew only too well. "I hear you and I know

how you are feeling." He walked to the sink, washed his hands, and then moved to the fridge and took out the package of steaks.

"Do you need help?" she asked.

"No, you sit down. I have some wine or beer, if you'd like. I may even have some iced tea. What would you like?" He stepped around the kitchen island, pulled out the oak swivel chair and motioned for her to take a seat.

She smiled at him as she sat down. "I'll take a beer. I'm pretty low maintenance."

He grabbed a Yellow Jacket out of the fridge and popped open the can and handed it to her. "I hope you like Banquets."

She took a swig. "Perfect. These are Matt's favorites, so I've learned to like them, too. The last time we were in Casper, my buddies ended up building an entire pyramid out of these damned things. It was awesome until some idiot, a bronc rider, decided to take a dive into it. He ended up cutting his arm and needing forty-five stitches. It really was a cool pyramid. We were going to send pictures into Coors and ask them to be our sponsors." She laughed.

"There's no way they could have turned you down if you had a performance like that." He smirked. "You never told me how you did on the circuit. You must have been pretty good. How many years were you doing it?"

She played with the tab on the can, making a thrumming sound as she let it go. "I was number three on the WPRA list of best barrel racers, and my total winnings my last year were well over a hundred and twenty thousand. I'd like to say it was me, but really, I had a fantastic gelding who was doing all the hard work. He was voted horse of the year."

"What is his name?"

"His working name is MacGyver Moonflash, but I just call him Mac. He is fun to watch—he's fast and agile. His lines are pure art."

"Do you still have him?"

She nodded. "Yeah, but I think it's a disservice to him. I think he could have still had a couple of good years running the circuit. I feel guilty. He loved his job. I've been thinking about selling him, but he is my best friend."

"Is he happy at the ranch?"

She tapped on the can. "I think so. I've been using him to work. Not so much barrel racing, but I do let him cut cattle. Well, we've been working on it. It's a new skill for him, but he definitely has it in his blood. He is taking to it naturally. You should see his pivot."

"Anytime you want to bring me out to the ranch, I'm game," he said, taking spices out of the cabinet over the stove and prepping the steaks for the grill. "And, for the record, I think Mac is probably just fine with you on the ranch. If you wanted, you could probably hire him out to stud and make a good living."

"I've talked to Matt about that."

He felt a wiggle of jealousy, though he knew it was senseless. Just because she was friends with Matt didn't mean there was anything or would be anything between them—and he wasn't in a position in which he was to worry about her; they were only friends. However, he wasn't the kind of friend she told him Matt was; he did want more.

He felt ridiculous for being jealous at a time like this. It was out of character for him, but maybe with everything that had happened over the last year, he had changed. Maybe that *life* thing had affected him more than he cared to admit.

"Are you going to stay around here, or do you think you are just going to stay at the ranch until you are back on your feet?"

She took a long drink of her beer and sat it back down on the counter with a thud. "Asking me my plans is like asking what the clouds will do next. I am the first person to admit that I can be a bit flighty."

Did that mean if he got close to her that she would leave him just like Haven had?

Now he wasn't so sure he wanted to open up to her and tell her what had happened. If he did, he would only make himself vulnerable and more apt to be hurt. He didn't need any more pain in his life—and neither did Jamie. They'd both had more than their fair share, not just in the last few years, but in their lives. It seemed as though both of their lives had been filled with incredible losses.

It was a wonder she had even agreed to come back to his house with him, that she had trusted him enough to be alone like this. Perhaps that was a good sign, one that indicated she wasn't going to run away. Yet he'd always followed the adage that when a person told you who they were, it was best to believe them.

It made him wonder how he would have explained himself—reclusive, jaded, unwilling to open up. If that were all true, was it really fair of him to have invited her back to his place and hope for a more romantic evening? Then he realized, if that were true, he wouldn't have invited her there, at all.

Perhaps what a person said about themselves was far harsher and more self-deprecating than was justified or accurate.

He knew only too well that he was his own worst critic.

Actually, that may have been Haven right up until she'd left—she had loved to point out all his faults and to use them against him.

"You went somewhere." Jamie stood up and walked over to him as he stared out the window and toward the lake. She put her hand on his lower back and the action and warmth was so soft and unexpected that he tensed for a moment before relaxing.

When he did, Jamie's face softened. "Are you okay?" she continued.

He nodded and turned to her. She kept her hand on his back and, as he moved, she wrapped her other arm around him as well. Her touch made his pulse race.

He wiped off his hands and then reached up and pushed a strand of hair from her face. "Do you have any idea how beautiful you are?" He smiled at her as he looked into her eyes.

"Thank you." Jamie grinned but didn't look away co-quettishly as some women would have done. She was so strong. "I have to tell you, from the first time I saw you on the mountain, I have been imagining what a moment like this with you would feel like."

He leaned down and his lips found hers. As his tongue grazed her bottom lip, he pulled her harder against his body. He slid his hand down her back and the other to the base of her head and slipped his fingers into her soft, thick hair.

Her breath caught as he took their kiss deeper, more fervent and wanting. He had wanted her, too. She had come out of nowhere and barreled into his life like hell on wheels and he loved her for it, he needed her—he needed her to bring him back to reality and to show him how it felt to be whole again.

She leaned away and looked at him. Her eyes were heavy with desire, and he couldn't help himself and he kissed her again, faster and hungrier.

Her fingernails dug into his skin as she kissed him hard. He didn't know who was in control and he didn't care.

She tasted like beer and want.

She let go of him and put her hand to his face.

As her thumb caressed his scruff, he broke their kiss. His body needed a moment for him to gain control. She was so sexy. He wanted her so badly.

"You...you are perfect." His voice was raspy and heavy with desire.

She laughed and looked away as she gently pulled free of his arms. Jamie licked his kiss from her lips, the action so unexpectedly sensual that he found himself wanting to pull her into his arms and kiss her again.

How dare she remove his kiss from her skin? He wanted to be there, to remind her of him for as long as he could...

At least until he told her the truth.

The truth... The thought pulled him to dinner. To why they'd come here and what he had promised her. He needed to be honest. Then, if he was, she could make an informed decision between staying or going. He wouldn't begrudge her if she decided his baggage was too heavy and his life was too much for her to want to even dip her toes into.

He turned to the counter and pulled out two potatoes and, cleaning and poking them, threw them into the microwave. He started it with a few pushes of the buttons and it hummed to life, filling the space between them with much-needed sound—and something besides his intrusive and damning thoughts.

Jamie took a long drink of beer and she closed her eyes

like she was trying to capture the flavor on her tongue forever.

"The beer isn't that good," he teased, grabbing some crackers out of the cupboard and sitting them on the counter in front of her for a snack.

"I wasn't thinking about beer. I was thinking about how glad I am to be here, and to be with you. And I'm trying to hold back my desire to tell you all the ways I'm not perfect—and trust me, there's a long list."

He smiled. "I'm so glad you are here, too. And as far as you being perfect, you may not be what you consider *perfect*, but some things are best in the eye of the beholder."

"Then you may need glasses." She giggled and the sound was so endearing and sweet that it made his chest tighten.

"If anyone in this room is imperfect, it is me," he said, grabbing a package of frozen corn kernels out of the freezer, pouring them into a pot with water and putting them on the stove, setting them to simmer.

"So far, I haven't seen anything that would give me any inclination to worry," she said with a smile.

Pierce gave an internal groan, but there was no doubt that his moment had come—he had to tell her the truth. "I have a past and I've made so many mistakes." He considered grabbing a beer but stopped himself in case she told him she wanted to leave and he had to give her a ride back to her truck. He didn't want to have any reason to keep her from leaving him and this place if what he told her disgusted her.

"Oh?" she asked, pulling a paper towel off the roll sitting in the middle of the counter with a tearing sound. "Have you bedded a thousand women? Should I call you Don Juan? Or do you have so many dating apps that your phone has run out of storage space from all your pictures and videos?" She gave him a cute look from under her brows as she sat back down on the chair and waited for the heavy blow of his admission to fall.

It was as if Jamie knew he was going to drop some kind of ax.

He hated that it had to be to the neck of their new relationship. "I'm not a fan of Lord Byron nor his Don Juan," he said with a laugh. "I'm a long way from a womanizer. In fact, for the last four years, I've only had one woman in my life. Her name was Haven—and today was supposed to be our wedding day."

There was a long deathly silence—the only sound was the hum. That damned hum.

He waited for Jamie to say something, but he didn't know exactly what he wished she would say or do. He didn't want pity. Heck, he didn't want to talk about the fact he should have been standing in a tuxedo in front of a church in Missoula, nearly at this moment. He didn't want to tell her he was still paying off the trip to London and through the UK. A trip he was supposed to now either take or eat the cost of—either way, he was paying for two tickets.

Mostly, he didn't want to tell her how badly losing everything that was supposed to be his past, present and future had broken him. Until now and meeting Jamie, he wasn't sure why he'd kept working so hard and pushing. It would have been so easy to just succumb to his desire to run away to Mexico and live on a beach.

Jamie reached over and took his hand with hers. "Is she still alive?"

Of all the ways he thought she was going to go with his admission, this had been the last one—and yet, he should have guessed. "She is." He nodded as he laced his fingers through Jamie's and gave her a look of apology for her loss. "But she's with another man—my half brother, Dylan."

She looked at him like he was on some '90s midday soap opera.

He definitely felt as though that is what his life had become. The torrid relationship had split his family down the middle. "After my mother passed when I was a teenager, my father remarried when I was a freshman in high school. I liked his wife, but her son Dylan and I never really got along."

"Ever?"

"We are the same age. Our birthdays are a day apart. One year, our parents tried to do a joint family party and it ended up with him and me in a fistfight—he started it. I am not one for that kind of violence. I ended up breaking these two teeth," he said, pointing to his front incisors. "He said my mother dying was the best thing that ever happened to me. I was lucky to have a stepmother like his mom. She was more than my father deserved."

"So, he literally asked for the fight?"

He nodded. "I didn't throw the first punch." He sighed, running his tongue over the smoothness of his crowns on his front teeth. "We never spoke again. Haven was our go-between while we were planning the wedding and all the events around it. His two kids were supposed to be our flower girls."

"Is he married?"

"He is now going through a divorce." He cringed at the truth of his dysfunctional family continued to unfold. "This is why I hate talking about all of this."

She lifted their entwined hands and her warm breath

caressed his fingers. Jamie dropped her forehead to their hands and paused for a moment before looking up at him. "You don't have to worry about me judging you for your family's actions. Regardless of what happened between you and this woman, you didn't push her into the arms of your stepbrother. She is an adult and made her choices. She, alone, is responsible for them."

"Some bridges are too far for respectful people and respectful families, and I understand that. Your family has a name in this community."

"My father ruined that name. You and I both know that. And regardless of what people think of my family, that has no relevance on my relationships. I will date whomever I want to date. I've spent enough of my time oppressed by my father and by the rules of society. I don't want anyone or any stupid unspoken standards running my life."

He pulled her to the edge of her chair and she wrapped her legs around him. The microwave beeped loudly and she turned and started to speak, but he took her by the chin. "No. Now you don't get to let a microwave dictate what we do, either."

He took her lips in a loving kiss. She really was everything he had been looking for; he'd always wanted a woman who would stop at nothing to get what she wanted and would say exactly what she was thinking and feeling. He appreciated directness—even though he knew it could be a double-edged sword.

Her hands moved to the edge of his shirt and he leaned into her, only too happy to oblige her bidding. She was everything in his world that mattered and the reason he wanted to breathe.

She pulled the fabric free of the confinement of his jeans

and the cool air rushed over the warm skin of his abs, chilling him and making goose bumps rise. He took her face in his hands and looked into her eyes, trying to thank her and tell her all the things that he could not say—all the things he was feeling and couldn't even put into words in his soul.

Her fingers skimmed over the muscles on his stomach and she dug her nails into his skin just hard enough to make temporary, delicious marks. She must have known how much he loved the edges of pain. "As much as I want you," she whispered, breaking their kiss but allowing their lips to graze as she spoke, "I don't think we should take things to the bedroom tonight. Not tonight. Not *this* night. I'll stay at your place tonight, but we can't sleep together. I don't want our first night together to be tainted by memories."

She could no longer argue; she was his definition of perfection.

Chapter Ten

Jamie had spent the night staring at the ceiling in Pierce's bedroom. The ride back to her pickup had been cordial but not chatty, and she had been grateful. Things between them weren't awkward, but they weren't what they had been the night before and, when she'd walked into the ranch house, she was grateful to take off her cowboy boots, sit down on the leather couch and turn on the television.

There were the sounds of someone in the kitchen and the smell of hot coffee, but she didn't say anything in hopes that whoever was up and moving hadn't heard her try to sneak into the ranch house this morning. She didn't want to answer any questions—no matter who asked.

The news was depressing and it cast a shroud on her thoughts and memories of her time with Pierce. His kiss had been so…so *powerful*.

It wasn't like anything she'd experienced before.

She had thought she had known passion and want, but what she felt with Pierce was so different.

It was so strange and unexpected that she wasn't sure it could be real. Perhaps it was just the ice breaking on her heart and the feeling of it starting to beat again. After everything he had told her last night, it had been no wonder he had been hesitant in bringing her into his life and in wanting to tell her the truth about his life and his past. From an objective point of view, he was a walking red flag.

And yet it wasn't his fault. He wasn't behind the horrible things that had happened in his life. She'd told herself she wouldn't judge him and to do so would have been victim-blaming at its worst.

With everything that had happened to him, though, she had to be concerned whether he was healed enough to move forward and find love again—especially with her.

In fact, she had to ask the same of herself.

If Pierce was the man she thought he was, he was probably asking himself that exact question. She was as broken as he was—two hearts that were as busted as theirs had no business moving as quickly as they were.

They needed to step back and take a moment to assess whether what they were feeling was real or if they were merely connected through kindred experiences and communal pain.

Matt came walking out of the kitchen carrying two cups of coffee. He sat it on the table next to her and then plopped down in the chair beside the couch. "Long night?"

"Can you tell?" She picked up the mug and took a sip of the hot creamy coffee. "Thank you for this, I needed it."

"You look like you went through it, and not in the best way." Matt leaned back. "If you want, I can make some breakfast. If you're trying to work off a hangover, there's nothing like a couple of eggs."

She shook her head. "Not a hangover, just a confusing night." She wasn't sure she wanted to tell Matt where she had been or with whom—she didn't want him to think she was sullying John's memory for even a second or moving on too quickly.

Besides, things with Pierce were in the very early stages. After their quiet drive home this morning, it was quite possible that they were through. Maybe he'd spent his night as she had, second-guessing his actions and wondering why he had made the choice to kiss her.

"You wanna talk to me about it?"

She sighed.

"Got it." Matt clicked back the recliner.

Jamie appreciated Matt's ability to read her and work around her tender areas. Maybe he would be fine with her dating again and it was just she who wasn't entirely ready to put words to whatever was happening in her life.

"I talked to your brother and Emily last night. Sounds like she is amped about rolling out on the investigation. She isn't up yet, though." Matt glanced down at his watch. "I think she has to head in soon."

She hadn't thought about it, but Pierce likely had a very long day ahead if he was heading the joint task force and leading the investigation. He would have to pull in resources from around the area and orchestrate well-organized searches of the complete death scene as well as take a deep dive into the mayor's life and disappearance. And that was just to start.

The thought of what it would take to command the unit was impressive, to say nothing about the volume of information they would pull together as a cohesive unit.

She didn't envy the work he had to do today. Organizing people was a nightmare. She would always prefer animals to people.

Emily walked down the hallway, adjusting her belt. Looking up, she spotted them. "You pour some coffee for me?"

"I'll grab you one," Matt said, putting down his recliner and going to the kitchen.

Emily sat down next to Jamie on the couch and grabbed her hiking books and started to put them on. "So, I was talking to your friend, Ranger Hauser. It sounds like he was interested in continuing the search of the mountain for more evidence. I'm going to run up there. If you are looking for a way to help, you are welcome to join."

"Is Pierce going to be up there with you?" she asked before she thought about what she was saying or how she must have sounded to Emily.

Her sister-in-law looked at her with a quirk of the brow.

Jamie looked away before Emily could see any tells on her face. She was a good detective, and probably good enough that even without looking at her, she had an idea of exactly what was happening. Jamie didn't need to give her any more information.

"I don't think he is hiking up to the mountain today. He is going to be incident command." Emily tied her boots and stood up. "Why don't you go ahead and ride with me up there? You can tell me about everything you know and catch me up."

Matt walked out of the kitchen carrying a to-go cup of coffee for Emily as Jamie stood up. She wasn't sure if she should stay or go, but there was nothing around here that Matt couldn't handle—he could handle feeding the horses and work with the ranch hands to check on the cattle.

As for going, things with Pierce had ended so quietly this morning. She pulled out her phone and looked to see if he had texted her—there was nothing. At minimum, she would have expected a "Thanks for last night" or "Have a good day." She wasn't about to be the one to reach out first. She wasn't thirsty.

If he hadn't texted, maybe she had been right about him regretting everything—or maybe she was just being neurotic and overthinking. It wasn't like he owed her anything and, even if they never spoke again, they had shared some amazing time together.

His kiss...

That had been one of the best kisses of her life. It was the only kiss she could even recall. When his lips had moved over hers, she had forgotten the world around her. Her hair had curtained her view of the world and there was only him and his kiss.

If she could, she wanted to see if she had the same feeling of weightless euphoria that she'd had before. If she did, then he and the relationship were something worth delving into, but more than likely, he had just been hurting.

She was his soft landing, a safe woman to keep from thinking about where he should have been and who he should have been with. Part of her wanted to see this woman. Yet, if Jamie never heard about her again, that would be entirely fine as well.

One thing was certain, she wasn't going to compete with a memory—and she wasn't going to make him compete with a ghost.

To bring her to his home, a home he may have shared with that woman, bothered her. Then again, the house hadn't looked like it had been worked over by a woman. If anything, it had looked as if a second-hand store had been giving furniture away and he'd taken what was left over at the end of the day.

She laughed at the thought. Maybe she wasn't so upset, after all.

Matt touched her shoulder. "You all right?"

She nodded. "I'm gonna run back up to Glacier and the investigation. Emily wants my help."

Matt looked over to her and she gave him a reaffirming nod.

She patted his hand. "Don't worry, man. I need to get out of the house and get my mind off things. This will be good for me. Would you mind tending to the animals for me? Make sure Mac is fed?"

"No problem. When I'm done, I may run into Kalispell and pick up some things at the store. I'll see you later."

"Sounds good. You know where the keys are for the ranch trucks." She motioned toward the board where all the keys were hung. "And, hey, thanks for the coffee."

He smiled widely. "Not a prob."

She followed Emily outside and to her blacked-out SUV. It was an undercover rig and it was badass. Jamie hadn't had the chance to ride in it before and she had a niggle of nerves as she stepped up to the door. It wasn't every day that she got into a cop car. As long as she got out, sans handcuffs, she would be fine.

As they drove toward the park, she told Emily about everything that had happened—from her rescue of Anthony to the cat's bluff charge.

"That's impressive. You've been through the wringer. I'm glad Ranger Hauser seems to have taken you under his wing," she said. "I don't know him very well, but it seems like he has taken to you. Yes?"

Oh, here came the twenty questions from the detective. She hadn't wanted to open up to Matt, and she'd known him far better than Emily, but Emily also hadn't been close to John. That wasn't to say she wouldn't judge her, but she had a feeling Emily had probably heard just about everything. Her talking about her emotions wasn't going to throw her sister-in-law for a loop.

"He has been good to work with. He's let me help, which has been cool."

Emily nodded, but she could see her looking over at her. "You know that isn't an everyday thing, right?"

"Yes." She didn't want to elaborate.

Emily smiled knowingly. And just like that, Jamie knew she had been caught.

"Is that where you were last night?"

There was no avoiding the conversation now. "Yes. It was supposed to be his wedding day. Nothing happened."

Emily's foot slipped on the gas pedal and the SUV lurched slightly. "His *wedding* day?"

"Exactly. He's a walking red flag."

Emily grumbled something unintelligible, but she could tell that Jamie was as bothered by the idea as she was.

"It was a bad breakup and not his fault. It's been a while since they have been together."

Emily's jaw unclenched, but only slightly.

"His family has about as much drama as ours."

Emily pulled to the side of the road after they passed through the front gates of the park. "Look, if you don't want to see Pierce ever again, I will take you back to the ranch right now. There is nothing here that requires your presence. I asked you here, admittedly, to try and get you to move things forward with him. After what you told me, maybe I screwed up."

It felt like an impasse—a choice between what could be and the end of complicated.

Jamie picked at her thumbnail. "I don't know if I *will* see him, but if I do, I don't mind. Just because he has a past doesn't mean I have any room to judge him. I have a past of my own. Most dudes would consider me a red flag, too."

Emily shook her head. "I highly doubt that—at least not when it comes to your past. They would probably judge you more for being a barrel racer. You know." Emily laughed.

Jamie stuck her tongue out at Emily and chuckled.

Emily pulled back onto the road and out into the line of traffic heading into the park. "You do what you think is right for you. If you think you are ready, don't let anything or anyone stand in your way."

"I appreciate that, sister."

Emily smiled. "You don't know how much that means to me. I was hoping we would get there someday. I wasn't sure how things would go with your family—or with you and your sister. Your brother said you were good people."

"I am," she said, tipping her head with grace. "I can't speak for my sister though."

"One step at a time. Considering your brother and I have only been together a year, I'd say things have come a long way in a short time."

"I think that just goes to prove how wrong we can be about people. Life and relationships are so complicated."

Emily nodded as she drove. "You don't have to tell me about that, I'm only too familiar. I don't know how much your brother has told you about how we got together, but it's a good whisky story."

The white incident command trailer was parked at the now-closed trailhead and a ranger was posted there to turn away any tourists who thought it a good idea to bypass the signs and enter at their own risk. As they parked, a woman in a burgundy Patagonia jacket, khaki shorts and a fanny pack with bear spray and two water bottles was standing in front of the man. She was leaning on two black trekking poles as though she was going to be hiking to the North Pole and not a well-kept and traveled trail.

Jamie could tell, based on the woman's scowling face, that she wasn't impressed that she was being turned away from the trailhead. The woman reached into her fanny pack and was drawing out her wallet, but the ranger was waving her off from what appeared to be a bribe.

There was a sign to the right of the ranger warning of the dangerous mountain lion and the recent interactions with humans, but apparently this woman must have thought something like that didn't apply to her. It was always this type of disconnect and apathy that created dangerous situations.

Regardless, Jamie was glad that they had decided to close the trail. If only they had taken it seriously earlier. At least no one else had really gotten hurt.

As Emily parked, she turned one last time to Jamie. "I'm going to leave this car open. If you don't want to stay around Pierce, or if the investigation becomes too much, you're welcome to find respite here."

Jamie nodded appreciatively. She said nothing as she got out, hoping that there would be no need for her to even think about running away or hiding. She could work with Pierce on the investigation without taking things to the next level in their relationship. They had no relationship, when it came right down to it. They were merely friends, and perhaps friends who kissed—maybe just that one time, last night.

It was amazing, but they both needed time before jumping any deeper.

Thinking about him, as though the simple act was some cosmic magnet, Pierce stepped out of the trailer and immediately looked in her direction. He smiled as he saw her. She smiled back, but it wavered on her lips as she thought about all the reasons they shouldn't be together.

A Black man stepped out of the trailer behind Pierce and tapped him on the shoulder, and he turned away. The man was wearing a ranger's uniform, but she hadn't seen him before. The two men were talking animatedly, and she could hear Pierce say something about Reynolds.

There was something about the way Pierce said the name that told her there were things the two men were unpacking when it came to their boss—and that relationship.

"We'll continue this later," Pierce said under his breath to the man as he turned to face them. "Hi, ladies. Jamie, I'm glad you came out—I wasn't sure you would."

So, he had felt the coolness between them this morning, as well. At least she wasn't alone in her assumptions.

"Hey, Vince," Emily said, sending a small two-fingered wave.

Jamie wasn't sure why she was surprised; of course Emily would know the rangers from the area. This probably wasn't the first time they'd worked together. Jamie was the newcomer here, not these folks.

"This is my sister-in-law Jamie," Emily said, introducing her. She noticed her gaze moving over to Pierce, but he seemed to look everywhere but at Emily, as if he could guess they had been talking. "She is considering joining my search and rescue unit."

Jamie tried not to act surprised.

Vince nodded as he walked over and extended his hand in greeting. "I'm a bit of a hugger," he said as she shook his hand and he pulled her into a gentle one-armed hug, their hands still clasped. "It's okay, you don't have to fake anything with me. Pierce already told me he has a thing for you. Just so you know, he is an awesome guy," he whispered, stepping back and sending her a wink.

Regardless of how much Vince liked him, when she stepped back, Pierce didn't seem to be able to meet her eye. Apparently, after last night, the best she could hope for in his life was an ancillary, accidental smile and promises of awkwardness.

Chapter Eleven

Pierce wanted to curl up under a rock and disappear.

He had made a major misstep in bringing Jamie to his house last night and there was no justification for his mistake. Of course, she would want nothing to do with him after that. The only surprise was that she'd come back to help with the investigation. However, according to Emily, she was thinking about joining SAR and her being there had nothing to do with him and more to do with her.

He could understand her desire to see this case through to the end. He regularly had to help with situations and disturbances within the park—especially partner and family member assaults in which he issued tickets or warnings but was then forced to leave the scene without really knowing what would come of his interceding.

In most cases, he had a feeling all he had done was make things worse. When women were victims of narcissistic abuse and domestic violence, a ranger or police officer coming in and writing tickets for the abuser's behavior would only escalate the danger.

At least for Jamie, she didn't have to worry about the violence continuing or worsening—well, hopefully. He hadn't heard from the medical examiner yet. If it was found that the mayor had died from anything more than a self-inflicted gunshot wound, then perhaps they did need to worry.

An ache rose in his gut.

He needed to make that call this morning. The results should be in today.

Vince motioned for him to step into the incident command trailer.

"Yeah?" he said, walking in and closing the door behind himself.

Emily and Jamie were standing outside. According to Emily, they were waiting for several other members of the SAR team. He was glad they were finally running at full capacity with the support of Reynolds. Even though everything was going the way it should, he had a sinking feeling he couldn't quite explain—and he didn't think it was entirely to do with the tension with Jamie.

Vince plopped down on the desk chair and it squeaked loudly under his weight. "Look, you and I both know Donovan was an ass. He had a reputation as a playboy and any one of his many girlfriends—or their husbands—could have been behind his death."

"You know how this goes. Everyone dies. It is just up to us to figure out the circumstances, not the justification or the righteousness. If we started to question if deaths were fair, we wouldn't be able to do this job."

Vince huffed a laugh. "That's no lie. All I'm saying is that maybe Cap was right in not pulling out all the stops for this one."

"He didn't know the ID when he was calling us off," he pointed out.

Vince raised a brow. "Oh?" He reached for an open bag of jerky and grabbed a piece. He pulled at the meat like he was some kind of scavenging bird. "You do know that Mayor Donovan was sleeping with Reynolds's wife?"

Pierce stopped. Vince had to be messing with him. "How do you know that? Is that just gossip or do you know something?"

Vince shrugged. "It was word on the street. Also, according to what I heard, the mayor's wife, Carey, was sleeping with any seemingly high-brow official she could get into bed. She was a social climber and would stop at nothing to succeed—even if that meant spreading her legs. I think she also wanted justice for Donovan's indiscretions—an eye-for-an-eye kind of thing."

"I only knew he had filed for a divorce, I didn't know anything about his wife. Or, their *situation*."

Vince nodded. "It gets better. What she couldn't get done with sexual favors, she gossiped about. She was notorious for running smear campaigns. She was one of the most toxic people I've ever met, and I gotta say Donovan would have been lucky to be rid of her."

"Was their divorce finalized when he went missing?"

Vince shoved the rest of the piece of jerky in his mouth and pulled open the laptop on the counter. He opened up the NCIC, or the Information Center, and typed Donovan's name. There was the complete list of everywhere he had ever lived, every phone number he'd been assigned, his social security number, and every single relative and relationship that could be used to track a person down.

The database was impressive, and as they dug around, they located Carey's information with a few simple clicks. According to what they found, the divorce had never gone through. However, she *had* filed a death certificate as she had an affidavit declaring he was suicidal and therefore he could be assumed dead.

That was interesting.

The marital property was still in probate and no ruling had yet been made. There was no information about the upcoming court appearance, but if there had been a filing, there would be a definitive date.

If there were any filings made now that they had found the body, and if there was any indication this was a homicide, they could file an injunction to stop the proceedings.

They needed answers, and fast.

There was no definitive proof that Carey was behind Donovan's death or disappearance, and it was very possible that her affidavit was correct, but there was something in Pierce's gut that told him there was more to this than Clyde just going to the woods and offing himself.

"Clyde was stepping out on his marriage, too. Do you know anything more about that?" he asked Vince.

Vince shrugged. "I only knew about Nicole, Reynolds's wife, for sure—Reynolds let it slip once. I can ask around at the courthouse, I have friends over there, but you might be best off just asking his dad, Judge Donovan. Or, you could talk to Emily. She worked in the same building and rubbed shoulders with the guy, I bet."

He nodded, but as he thought about talking to Emily his mind instantly moved to Jamie.

Maybe having her here wasn't a good thing. Everything he did seemed to make him think of her—she had become a distraction. That wasn't fair of him, and he had a feeling her being there or twenty miles away was irrelevant. He would be thinking about her regardless of her location.

Things between them had gone sideways because of him.

She hadn't done anything wrong—in fact, she had been right and the sensible one. He had apologized, but there was really no coming back from the major mistake he had made. Or maybe the fact that she was here and *wanted to* be here, meant that he had some room for redeemability.

"Don't worry about her." Vince smiled.

"Huh?"

"I can see you're thinking about Jamie," Vince teased. "Just do what you do best and be your charming self. She wants you, man." Vince stood up and cuffed him playfully on the shoulder. "Just maybe not on what was supposed to be your wedding night. Dude, that was amateur hour. At least, you shouldn't have told her."

"Just because you hide things from the women you date doesn't mean I do."

"Clearly, you've been out of the dating game for a while," Vince said with a tired laugh. "If you started telling everyone the truth, dating would go nowhere. You have to play the game a little bit, man."

Pierce had no game. That was a fact. Plain and simple, he didn't want to have game. He just wanted to find a good woman who respected him and didn't leave his heart shredded in the dirt.

If Jamie would give him another chance, maybe they could take things as they came and keep trying. They had so much in common and when he saw her, just like today, every part of his body lit up. It was like she was a sunbeam in the darkest of winter days.

"The closest thing I have to game is watching college football," he joked, stepping to the door. "If you manage to pull anything else about Donovan, let me know."

"Actually," Vince said, rubbing the back of his neck nervously, "I want to tell you before it comes out any other way…"

"Did you date Emily or something?"

"Not Emily…" Vince gave him the guiltiest look he had ever seen him give. "Around the time Donovan went missing, his wife and I might have been having a *thing*."

He stopped with his hand on the door handle. Vince was his best friend and the man who was supposed to have been the best man at his wedding. He knew his buddy had a habit of bedding just about any woman who would take him, but this was a new low.

Pierce turned back to Vince and looked him square in the face. "You had better hope that the medical examiner comes back with a report that says there is no way this was a homicide. If they don't, you know you will be off this investigation…and will instead be put on the top of our list of suspects."

Chapter Twelve

Pierce came out of the incident command trailer a different man than when he had walked in. Even his gait had changed. When he stepped out, he was on a mission, and he charged toward Jamie, took her by the arm and led her to his truck. "You're coming with me."

She looked over her shoulder in Emily's direction, who sent her a look of concern. Jamie shook her head and mouthed, *It's okay*. Emily frowned, but she gave her a nod and motioned for her to call.

It was strange, but the way Pierce had just taken control of her and the situation was a kind of a turn-on. She liked that he didn't ask questions or want to dance around the issues anymore. Whether or not he wanted to talk about what had happened, he wanted her with him.

He walked her to his truck and opened the door. "We have to run some errands. Get in."

She could tell it wasn't a suggestion and she stepped up and settled in. As he got in and they headed out, she wanted to ask him what had happened inside that little white trailer, but based on his scowl, she wasn't sure she wanted to roll the dice. He looked as though he was jonesing for a fight.

After a few minutes of driving, Pierce picked up his phone and dialed. "Dr. Lee? Hey, yeah."

She couldn't really make out the words, just the baritone of the man's voice on the other end of the line.

Pierce asked a series of questions, but she didn't really track what the conversation was about besides the status of the remains and that he must have been on the phone with someone from the crime lab. From what she could make out, they weren't going to drive all the way to Missoula to see the remains again, but the doctor would be sending all the findings via email.

As they spoke, Pierce's expression darkened, and his frown deepened so much that it shaded his eyes and made them appear almost black. The effect was almost frightening.

He sped down the highway as he listened to the doctor. It wasn't until they were near to the city of Kalispell that he finally hung up the phone. The sun was breaking through the morning clouds and the fog was rolling off the yellow canola fields as they sped through Evergreen and to the city.

She opened and closed her mouth, not sure what exactly to ask without overstepping her place. "Where are we going?"

He looked at her as though he had nearly forgotten that she was in the truck with him. It took him a long moment before he spoke. "I was hoping we could just go get some breakfast and I could talk to you about last night and set things right, but thanks to that call, our day is going to have to take a different turn."

"We don't need to talk about last night. We are fine." Her voice was thin, but she meant what she said, and she hoped he knew she was being authentic. "I want to get to know more about you, but let's take things one step at a time."

He smiled widely as he looked over at her and the darkness in his eyes mostly disappeared. "You have no idea how glad I am to hear you say that. I was so worried. I thought I'd screwed everything up last night. And this morning... I just didn't know what to say or do to make things right."

She reached over and extended her hand. "It's all good. I don't get things right most of the time. Let's just stick together."

He nodded and slipped his hand in hers and gave it a squeeze. "You really are an amazing woman. We'll take things as they come." While he had meant the words in the best way, a lump formed in his gut.

Anytime he had ever taken things as they came, and allowed fate to take control of his life, things had a way of going a whole lot of sideways.

He sent Emily a quick text message to let her know Dr. Lee was sending them his findings and to expect them in the next hour. With that, the rush he had been feeling abated. He was tempted to find and question the women in Donavan's life, but as things stood, they hadn't even delivered the official death notification.

"Are you hungry?" he asked.

Jamie giggled.

"What?" he asked, looking over at her with a smile.

"I should have guessed that taking things as they come would mean taking me to breakfast. You are such a dude sometimes." She tilted her head back slightly as she laughed.

THE SOUND WAS light and heady, and it was so clear and clean that it made the knot in his gut dissipate.

That sound, her, this, and the lightness—this was what he had needed, what they had *both* needed.

"Until we get the answers we need from Dr. Lee, namely a positive identification on the remains, there's not a whole lot more we can do. So let me take you to breakfast. I want to learn more about you. On my end, I want you to learn more about me. Then if you decide you don't want to have anything to do with me, it has nothing to do with my past and it has everything to do with me. At least you can make an informed decision." He tried to give her his best charming smile.

She giggled again. "You're really rolling the dice, you know that, right?"

He pulled his truck into a parking spot in front of Bojangles, a greasy spoon if there ever was one. The restaurant hadn't really changed since he was a kid. His parents had always brought him here on Sunday mornings after church. There was the same tired train set that ran around the crown molding of the ceiling.

The place always smelled like maple syrup and bacon, and this morning as they walked in, it had the heavy scent of burnt coffee. And a waitress motioned for them to take a seat wherever they liked. Pierce picked a faded and cracked-vinyl turquoise-colored booth by the front window where he could watch his pickup.

The waitress hurried over and, without asking, flipped over the mugs that sat on the table, and poured them two fresh cups of coffee. The woman was wearing blue jeans and a pink shirt with the name of the restaurant on it. Its plainness seemed perfectly in line with the rest of the restaurant. He actually liked it for exactly what it was—lacking any pretense.

"The menus are there on the end of the table," the waitress said, motioning to them. "Is there anything else I can get you to drink besides your coffee? The woman had obviously been doing this job for so long that she didn't even need to pause to think. Everything she seemed to do and say was on autopilot.

Pierce was almost envious. It would have been nice to have a job where everything was routine and fairly predictable. Plus, there was an honesty with her work. There was no vagueness or delving into the underbelly of human nature. She just came to work, did her job, and went home. Perhaps that was what he resented the most. There was no leaving his job at the door. It was his entire identity, just as barrel racing was Jamie's.

Walking away from that must have been so hard on her. He couldn't imagine how lost she must have felt choosing to leave that lifestyle. And from what he had gathered, she hadn't looked forward to coming back to the ranch.

He watched as she took a sip of coffee. He considered delving right into the topic of her loss, not only of her fiancé but of herself. Maybe their relationship could help her find new meaning in her life.

Then again, he didn't want to start a relationship on a cornerstone like that. That was a recipe for codependency, and it sounded so unhealthy. She needed to know and be comfortable in her own skin before adding him to her circle.

"You said you're helping your brother with the ranch. Is that what you plan on doing for the foreseeable future?"

Jamie shrugged. "I don't know what I want to do. I've actually been thinking about working with kids and horses. Doing some kind of equine therapy, or after-school program. But at the same time, I think that would be better when my life is more settled." She took another drink of her coffee.

He stayed quiet, and could tell from the look on her face that there was something more she wanted to say.

"Really, I'd like to go back to barrel racing. However, it just doesn't make sense. And I just don't know how to reconcile all the things I'm thinking about into a marketable career. I mean you and I talked about even studding Mac, but he's still a good horse and doing that kind of makes it sound like he's ready for retirement." She studied her fingers.

"And if he's ready for retirement, then you are, too?" He put his hand on her arm, trying to comfort her.

"Exactly." She put her hand on top of his and squeezed his fingers. "I'm too young and should just be *done*. I know I made the choice to walk away, but now that I'm in Montana and things are starting to calm down and I'm feeling better, I don't think I did it for the right reasons."

There was something in the way she spoke that sounded like healing. He loved it. It made him feel free to explore his feelings with her, and yet what she was saying was a little bit terrifying. If she wanted to run away and follow the rodeo circuit, she wasn't ready to settle down and he wasn't sure that he wanted a long-distance relationship. However, he wasn't sure he really wanted to have a settle-down-style relationship anyway.

If nothing else, they could just be hot messes together.

And perhaps he was wrong about the codependency thing, maybe healing together wasn't such a bad thing. Humans were always growing and changing, life wasn't static. If people waited for things to be perfect and unmarred, no one would ever be ready for relationship or friendship or to take things to the next level. Life was never flawless.

Now he was the one overthinking things. It struck him

as a little bit funny that this morning had started out with him telling her that they would take things as they came, and yet he was sitting there lashing himself with *what-ifs* and *why-nots* and *can'ts*.

The waitress rushed back over with a notepad in hand, ready to take their order. "You guys know what you're havin'?"

Neither of them had glanced at the menu, but when he looked to Jamie, she nodded. "I'll just get three pancakes, please."

"I'll do the same, with a side of bacon and two over-medium eggs."

"You got it, hun." The waitress jotted down their order and shoved the pen behind her ear. "It should be coming right up. Charlie's on the grill today, he's real quick." She looked around the restaurant, which was only about half full of what looked like regulars, mostly retirees who were off this time of the morning. "You should see it in here on the weekends during tourist season. It's a madhouse. I swear, there are times where I'd be better off just handing plates through the crowds to get them to the right tables. Ya know?"

"I work up in the park, I know all about the tourist season and how crazy things can get."

The waitress smiled at him, looking at his uniform and then down at the gun on his utility belt. "I assumed as much. I heard all about that bunch of bones you found up there yesterday. Sounds like you guys got your hands on the mayor. That true?"

His jaw dropped, but he tried to control his shock. He hadn't told anyone about what they had found, or whom. He had no idea how word had gotten out not only through

West Glacier, but all the way into Kalispell and into a tiny little diner in the middle of town. Kalispell was a city. That meant everybody knew what was going on in the park—potentially even Mayor Donovan's family.

If they had heard it through gossip, that would have been a horrible way to find out about their loved one's passing. It would look horrible for his department and the task force. His reputation was on the line for this case, and to have it blasted all over the Bojangles' pipeline was a problem.

"Right now, we can't really make any statements," Jamie said, taking the reins. "But we sure are looking forward to having a little breakfast. I appreciate you getting that order in." She sent the waitress an overly sweet smile that didn't leave room for further question.

As the waitress spun on her heel and hurried toward the kitchen, he leaned closer to her over the table. "Thank you."

She tipped her head in acknowledgment. "You need to work on your poker face."

"That right there is why I'm not much of a gambler. Don't take me to Vegas."

She smiled. "You know that there's other things to do in Vegas besides gambling?"

"If you mean the Little White Wedding Chapel, I've heard of it."

Her face pinkened. "That, and there are a ton of shows. I was down there for the NFR. We stayed at the South Point. You should try their spa. Oh my goodness, it's incredible—better than the Bellagio's."

He stared at her for a long moment and it struck him as such a strange juxtaposition of things—here they were in a run-down diner in the middle of a nowhere town talking about which spa was the best in the best and most expensive cities in America. He smirked.

"What?" She caught his gaze, playfully. "Would you get married at the Little White Wedding Chapel?"

He thought about the big wedding he was supposed to have had with hundreds of guests and all the pomp and circumstance that had been associated with the event. "Truth be told, I'd prefer it to the grandeur. With the right person, it's not about the event or all the *stuff*. For me, it was always about spending time with the people I love and celebrating the promises of forever." There was a sourness in his voice that he couldn't hide.

"So, you were going to have a big wedding?" She took a drink of coffee.

He nodded.

"Yeah, not my style, either. I'd do it at the ranch or in a chapel in Vegas—maybe even at the park, sans the mountain lion."

There was that laugh again. The one that cleared all the pain from his thoughts and the cobwebs from his soul. He would do anything to keep her making that sound—even if that meant they kept talking about weddings…a subject he had thought he'd never want to discuss again.

"You faced it down like a champ," he teased.

"You know, of all the things I would do with my life, I never thought having a mountain lion try and attack me would be on the list."

"True, but look at the bar stories you can tell now. You are a queen." He chuckled.

"I was a queen before," she teased, puffing up in her vinyl seat proudly. "I mean have you seen all this? I'm almost buff. I only get a little winded going uphill while hiking." She laughed loudly.

Yes, he loved that sound and maybe, if he was being honest with himself, he loved her, too. She was something special.

The waitress came over, carrying a stack of plates. "Here you go, guys. Syrup is there by the menus." She placed the plates down in front of them and motioned toward the three jars of syrup in the little carrying tray. The syrups were always the same—apricot, berry-something and maple.

As they settled in and smeared the little globes of butter over their pancakes, Jamie did a happy dance in her booth seat. He liked seeing her happy. It made him happy, too.

A few moments later, the waitress returned and refilled their mugs with piping hot coffee.

His phone pinged with a text message as she walked away. The email had shown up from the medical examiner. Unlocking his phone, he pulled up the encrypted document. There was a myriad of reports. He clicked through the osteology report and the anthropologist's findings.

According to their reports, it was concluded that the remains they had found on the mountain were, in fact, of a single person.

Thanks to the ID and the dental records they had pulled from the local dentist's office, they could safely presume that this individual was Clyde Donovan.

He had a positive identification.

As for the cause and manner of death, it was determined to be a gunshot wound to the left temporal lobe. From what they'd learned about Clyde, he was a right-handed individual. Therefore, based on this, the medical examiner had ruled the death as suspicious and yet to be determined. In short, this meant the ball was in his court.

Pierce stabbed the egg's yolk and let the yellow ooze out. There was nothing like reading a medical examiner's report over breakfast.

From the findings, it was likely that they had been correct in their initial assumption—they were dealing with a homicide.

Chapter Thirteen

Jamie was relieved everything had turned around between her and Pierce. Things could start fresh. Well, as fresh as it could get when they were dealing with death on their doorsteps.

Pierce's phone rang as they got into his pickup outside the diner. He looked over at her as he buckled up. "Vince was supposed to be my best man. He is a pretty good dude. A little screwed up sometimes when it comes to women and relationships, but I'm definitely not one who should be judging."

He answered and put the phone call on Speaker as he buckled up. "Hey Vince, what's up?"

"Hey, man, I saw the email." His voice sounded tired and drawn, like he was worried.

"Oh, good."

"You alone?" Vince asked.

Pierce glanced at her. "Actually, I'm sitting here with Jamie, you are on speakerphone. How come?"

There was a long pause. "You know that thing we were talking about earlier?"

"Uh-huh, why?" Pierce frowned.

"Can you please not tell anyone about that? I don't want

that getting out, given what they seem to think. You know what I mean?"

Pierce's frown deepened. "I do. I'll keep it under my hat as long as I can. In the meantime, I suggest you find something that keeps us from having to go there—got it?"

Jamie had no idea what they were talking about, but she felt like an interloper in their conversation, and she pointed toward the door, silently asking if she should step outside so they could take their conversation privately. Pierce shook his head.

"I just don't need anything to get out."

"We'll talk about this later. In the meantime, I'm going to go notify Clyde's family and wife about his death. I think, given the circumstances, I may have Emily meet me there. Is she there with you?"

"Yeah."

"Can you tell her to meet me there in thirty?"

"You got it, boss."

"The dogs on site?" he asked.

"Yeah, we are looking for the exact location where Clyde died. I think we are getting pretty close. Looks like he was near a large pine. I'll send you pictures of the scene."

"Great. Make sure you mark everything. Don't do anything without a sheriff's deputy working with you. We want to cover our bases in case this thing blows up, okay?"

Vince let out a nervous exhale. "Yeah. I hear you. Anything else?"

"Just be smart. Redundancy is better than absence of information."

"Yeah. I'll let you know how our search goes. Pictures will be coming your way as soon as we get everything narrowed down and the scene buttoned up. Talk to you later, bud."

"Later." Pierce clicked off the call. He stared out the windshield for a long time as though he wasn't sure what or how he should broach the awkwardness that had just planted itself between them. "So."

She waited, but he said nothing. "So." She lifted a brow. "You don't have to tell me the secret. Obviously, your friend doesn't want something to be talked about. I understand the need for secrets and boundaries in your line of work. If you want to tell me, cool, but don't feel forced."

He pinched his lips as he nodded plaintively. "He doesn't, but I could use an ear on how to deal with this thing."

Her heart leapt at the idea of him turning to her to be his sounding board. "Oh?"

"Whatever I share with you, it stays between us. I know it's probably not fair of me to ask you, but is that okay?"

She tried to control her excitement as she nodded. "Absolutely. I know how to keep a secret."

He started the engine of the truck and squeezed the steering wheel like he was fighting within himself whether he should talk to her about it or not. "Vince is more connected to this case than I would like. I don't want to pull him from the investigation just yet, as it would raise a lot of questions. Yet, if it comes out that he has anything to do with the death—it could cost me my career."

She didn't know the right thing to say, but what had been excitement was now only sourness in her stomach. "You are playing a dangerous game."

"Oh, you don't need to tell me. I love Vince—he and I have been friends for a long time—but he can do stupid

Mystery on the Range

things. However, when push comes to shove, he's always had my back and stood in my defense."

She smoothed her hair behind her ear as she tried to think.

"Hear me out," he continued. "Last year, I had a tourist file a complaint about a ticket I wrote. They had made it sound like they were saints and were helping an injured animal. While they were actually hazing a bear and trying to get a good picture for Instagram. Vince had watched the incident. If it hadn't been for him, and his statement, they would have gotten off and I would have been put on administrative leave for at least a week while Reynolds did a full investigation. The whole deal was incredibly stupid."

"I'm sure Vince is a great colleague and friend," she said.

"I know what you're going to say," he said, putting his hand up. "But I don't want to pull the rip cord and hand over the information just yet."

"Okay, but you know that you *should*."

He tilted his head back against the headrest. "I have to trust him on this. He said he didn't have anything to do with the guy's disappearance. I can't imagine that he would have had a role in the guy's death. Vince is my best friend, not a murderer."

She loved how loyal he was to his friend, even if she could tell he was lying to himself. She wasn't involved in law enforcement, but even she was aware that anyone could kill if they were faced with the right set of circumstances.

Regardless of what she thought, now was her opportunity to be as good a friend to him as he was to Vince and stand beside him while he needed support. "Look, if you think he is trustworthy and you are willing to stake your reputation and career on him, then that says something. But I think we need to move fast. We need to find out who would have wanted this guy dead."

"Exactly what I was thinking," Pierce said, looking over at her and sending her a relieved smile. "Clyde was known for being a narcissist."

"Well, he was a politician—doesn't that go hand in hand?"

He laughed. "I can't say I know any of them personally, but I'd have to assume you're probably right. They seem like the type." He put the truck in gear. "And I have to say, while I never enjoy giving death notices, this one should be interesting."

"Oh?" she asked as he pulled out of the parking space and got onto the main road.

"Clyde and his wife were in the process of a divorce. He had filed the paperwork, but nothing had been finalized when he had gone missing."

That *was* interesting. She'd always heard in situations like this, it was always the spouse who was investigated and suspected first. "When he went missing, was she questioned?"

He turned down a side road, leading them through downtown Kalispell, which consisted of a collection of charming Old West–style brick buildings with cloth awnings. "I'm sure, but I haven't talked to Emily about it."

"I went to school with a bunch of the Donovans. You know it's a pretty big name around the valley."

He raised a brow.

"Their family homesteaded the area in the late 1800s. They still have a bunch of cattle ranches and farms that stretch down south into the Flathead Indian Reservation and north almost all the way to the Canadian border."

"So, they are well-heeled?"

She nodded. "But that probably isn't a huge surprise. It takes money to get into politics here…well, *anywhere*." She looked at the courthouse, which sat in the middle of a wye in the road in the center of town. It was an oddly out-of-place building and obnoxious in the way it forced everyone to move around it and pay homage to its grandeur. "His father was the district court judge. In fact, I think he still is, but I don't know for sure. I haven't looked it up since I've been back to see if he was reelected."

It struck her as incredibly odd that a mayor, who was also the son of a district court judge, had gone missing and no one had taken the fall. She would have thought heads would have rolled. Maybe things had changed while she had been away, but she thought small-town justice—or warped vengeance—would never fail.

"Maybe that is where we should start," Pierce said excitedly, slamming on the brakes and turning the truck hard to the right. "Has anyone ever told you how beautiful and smart you are?" He smiled broadly at her.

"What?" she asked, grateful for the compliment but confused by his sudden shift.

"We have to do the death notifications, but there are no rules about who we have to notify first. Given the circumstances at the time of his disappearance, I think it is understandable if we talk to his father first." He sent her a smile. "While we are there, and if he wishes, we could ask him a few questions. Then we can meet up with Emily at the wife's."

Jamie loved this side of Pierce. He was filled with hope

and excitement for the future. It was strange and exhilarating, and it struck her that in his own right, while looking for justice, he had become a predator.

Chapter Fourteen

Pierce stared at the No Firearms sign on the glass of the courthouse's front door as he held it open for Jamie. The courthouse hadn't changed since the last time Pierce had been there to get his wedding license nearly a year ago. It still carried the heavy scent of stress, anxiety and fear in the air.

When he'd first come here, he couldn't understand why they had put the justice of the peace in a place like this— where so many people's real-life nightmares were exposed to the air and the public and set out to be judged not only by strangers, but also potentially by the media. A shiver moved down his spine as he thought of all the trials and convictions that had been wrought within these walls. He also thought of all those who had been guilty of horrific crimes and yet had walked free.

Maybe, given how his marriage license thing had turned out, as well as what they were here to look into, the justice of the peace being in such a place did make sense.

He gave a dark laugh.

If he wasn't careful, this darkness could easily turn bitter.

In the center of the courthouse was a round mahogany desk that was about waist high. It was decorated with carved filigrees and swirls, similar to the cast-iron banisters on the stairs leading upstairs to the courtrooms and offices. Behind the desk sat a security guard and he waved them down as they approached. "Hey, guys, how's it going?" He looked at Pierce's badge and his nameplate. "How can I help you today, Ranger Hauser?"

"We don't have an appointment, but I am here to speak to District Court Judge Donovan. Do you know if he's in his chambers, or in trial today?"

The guard glanced to his computer, but from where Pierce was standing, he could not see what the man was looking at, exactly. "I think his trial was delayed today. And it looks like he's in his chambers. Let me see if he's available. First, do you mind telling me what this is in regard to?"

When it came to meeting with a judge, it wasn't easy getting behind those doors regardless of whether he carried a badge or not. They were busy, and their time was precious. However, he had a feeling he held the golden ticket—he just had to be careful how much he told the security guard. Then again, even the waitress knew about who they had found in the woods. By now, it was a wonder that this guy wasn't telling Pierce about why he was there and just ringing him through. Maybe that was why he had waved him down instead of assuming he'd known where he was going.

"We are here regarding Donovan's son. We need to ask him a few questions. Time is of the essence." He kept his face unreadable.

Even if the gossip mill had run rampant, he wasn't going to feed it any more than was necessary.

The guard stared at him for a second too long, giving it away that he did, in fact, already know exactly why they were there and what they had found. It made Pierce wonder if there actually had been a newspaper article or something about what they'd discovered.

As the man turned to his computer and typed, it dawned on Pierce how everyone seemed to know everything—social media.

It wasn't that he was a Luddite; he used social media, too. It was just that he didn't use social media to get his news or to hear gossip. He used it to find funny pictures to send to Vince and his friends, but that was about the extent. In total, he probably spent twenty minutes a day watching stupid videos.

However, this guy, who sat behind a desk and waited for people to enter the courthouse each day, probably had a lot of free time. It was no wonder he knew what was going on.

"Judge Donovan said he will see you now. He will meet you outside his chambers." The guard stood up. Standing, he maybe pushed five feet, and Pierce couldn't help but notice that his gun didn't have a magazine racked and ready. "He is on the third floor, second door on your left. You can go in through the courtroom and his office is to the right. You will see when you get there. If you get lost, I can help."

"Thanks," Jamie said, smiling graciously, but Pierce noticed her gaze slip to the man's soup sandwich of a gun.

The way the man had his gun, if there was an emergency, the best thing he could do with the unloaded gun was throw it at the threat. As they turned away, Pierce tried to tell himself that maybe the guy had just taken the No Firearms sign to include him as well—sort of.

Jamie's boots clicked loudly on the marble floors of the foyer as they made their way to the stairs. The place carried the air of the 1800s in a way he couldn't quite put his finger on; perhaps it was the Western-style frescos of storming bison and cowboys carrying lever-action rifles on the domed ceiling overhead.

As they moved up the steps, he felt as if he should have been wearing something black with tails and carrying a monocle in his breast pocket. There was even a faint smell of pipe smoke, or maybe the scent was just in his imagination.

Jamie slid her hand on the black cast-iron banister as she moved up the stairs. "I forgot how cool this place was. It is beautiful."

He was surprised how differently they were experiencing this moment.

"Then again, it is a bit haunting—you know?" she asked, sending a look back at him over her shoulder.

"It's not my favorite place to be."

She caught his gaze, and her enjoyment seemed to falter. "Oh, I bet you are here a lot for work, huh?"

"Actually, no. I work for the federal government—this is all for state stuff."

"Oh, right." She turned back. "I should have known that."

He moved up to her side. "I try to stay out of courthouses—federal or otherwise." He grazed her hand with the back of his, trying to send her a tiny gesture to help her feel better. "There's a lot about your work and ranching that I don't know. Don't beat yourself up about it."

She smiled at him, a grateful softness in her eyes. Dammit if that look didn't make him melt. If she had asked him for the moon at that moment, he would have done anything to give it to her.

She grazed her fingers over his as she ascended the last

few steps to the third floor. "You've got this. Good luck."
She winked.

This was one thing he wasn't sure about—he probably
had a better chance lassoing the moon than prying information out of a man who made a living keeping secrets.

Emily hadn't sent him anything about the missing person's case, as they had only just confirmed the man's
identity. Maybe he should have waited to read up about
everything and all the statements that had been made about
the man in the past. However, this *was* just supposed to be
a notification.

Even if Pierce was there to question the judge about his
son's disappearance or life, he had a feeling that a judge
wasn't the kind of person who was just going to open up
and spill precious details.

He took a deep breath, preparing himself for whatever
he was going to face when he entered the second door on
the left. It was silly, but he was nervous. He had spent quite
a few days in court, having been subpoenaed on a myriad
of cases in which prosecutors had called him in after he
had been involved during the initial arrests. It was one part
of his job that he always despised. Maybe it was the lawyer thing. He'd yet to have met one that he could stomach.

He'd never liked a person whose loyalty was available
for purchase.

There was a solid wooden door with Lady Justice carved
into its surface. He pulled open the heavy door with its
glossy brass handle and waited for Jamie to step through.
Pierce was hit with the strong aroma of fear mixed with
industrial disinfectant and floor wax.

The courtroom was larger than he would have expected,
but much the same as every other he had been in within

this state—it had the same austere 1800's feel, thanks to its oak floors and whitewashed walls. It had leaded-glass windows that were opaque enough to let light in but obscure the views in and out. It was a disorienting space of professionalism and practicality.

Sitting in the middle of the empty courtroom, on the prosecution's side, was a gray-haired man. He was wearing a dark blue suit. He had his back to them, and he was tapping away on his cell phone, preoccupied with work.

As Pierce neared the man, he noticed that there was a hole worn in the seam of the right shoulder thanks to wear. The man turned with the sounds of the footfalls on the oak floor. "Ranger Hauser?" he asked, looking at Jamie and then to him.

"Yes, that's me. Judge Donovan?" he asked.

The man stood, stepped out from the bench seat and extended his hand to Jamie. "You are?"

"Jamie. Trapper," she said, taking the man's hand gently.

He cupped her hand and gave it a welcoming shake before doing the same with Pierce. He slapped him on the shoulder and motioned for him to sit down. "It's great to meet you, Ranger. I was wondering when I would get the knock on my door."

"I'm sorry we didn't get here sooner—before the rumors."

The judge sat down on the bench. He patted the seat beside him, the action strangely informal in what was an incredibly formal and stuffy room. Jamie sat down on the bench behind the judge, motioning with her chin for him to sit where the man had offered.

He slid into the seat, but he was so uncomfortable that he would have almost preferred to be sitting in the defendant's chair in active court.

"You know the thing about rumors..." the judge said, staring up at the bench. "They are often true, but they never hold up in court. It's not until we are slapped in the face with evidentiary support that we can assign legitimacy. In this case, I was sincerely hoping that the rumors were wrong."

Pierce didn't know what to say, but he had a feeling this man wasn't looking for a response.

The judge pressed a finger in the space between his brows, like he was staving off a headache. "That boy of mine was always hard to track. When he wasn't off chasing women, he was chasing ideas. Neither tended to be good for him."

He wanted to tell the judge that everyone knew men who were like that—they were typically the type A kinds with egos too big for their hats. Vince came to mind.

"When he married *that* woman, I tried to warn him off." He sighed. "He listened just about as well as he did when he was a teenager. I told him she was one of those things I wasn't going to be able to bail him out of—and that divorce was going to be expensive."

At least Pierce's assumptions of Carey had been right— she had a reputation as a woman who was not well received in the Donovan family or in the community.

"She was a terrible woman before she met him. I'd seen her in my courtroom before they met. She had a penchant for stealing identities for financial gain and then, and worse, embezzling funds from her father's business. Luckily, she had a good defense attorney, and she was just pretty enough to get the pity vote from jurors. If she hadn't, she would have still been sitting in prison—I would have seen to it. Instead, she got married to my son."

Pierce tried to control his shock. He could even imagine being in this father's position. He thought he'd had a family with some drama—this was another level entirely. However, it did increase the likelihood of Carey having played a role in Clyde's death tenfold.

"Even though she was found innocent, you do believe she was guilty of fraud?" Pierce asked.

The judge made a face and shrugged, and Pierce knew it was the closest thing he was going to get to a real answer from the judge. Anything else would constitute potential defamation if the man wasn't careful.

He was smart, but Pierce wouldn't say he was lucky.

His gaze moved to the hole in the man's suit. The guy had spent a lot of time in that suit, and probably others just like it. He'd likely spent more hours in that suit than he had with his own son when Clyde had been growing up. Maybe that was why Clyde had become the man he had—and why Clyde had chosen to become a mayor.

Maybe he had thought that in becoming a city official, he would finally get his father's much-coveted and hard-to-obtain attention.

Pierce didn't know whom he pitied more—the father or the son and the living or the dead.

Chapter Fifteen

The judge's deep-set and heavily bagged eyes would haunt Jamie for years to come; she held no doubt. The man had to have seen so many horrors in his line of business, but from his vacant expression, she could tell that he was struggling to remain composed. It was as if he was teetering on the edge of falling apart.

She had never had a child, but she could only imagine the pain and anguish that came with the undeniable knowledge that a parent was to never see them alive again. A parent was not supposed to outlive their child. That wasn't the natural order of things. It broke her heart to even think about it.

If the judge wanted to talk about his son or the impact his loss had on his family, he was free to do that, but she didn't feel as if it was her place to start the conversation. This interview, or notification rather, was Pierce's job.

Pierce stood up and extended his hand to the judge. "If you need anything, or if you can think of anything else that could be helpful in our investigation into your son's death, please don't hesitate to reach out. I'm working with Detective Monahan on the investigation, so you are free to call her or myself."

The judge shook his hand graciously. "I appreciate you

coming here and telling me face-to-face. This has been a long time coming, but news I expected. Don't let this bother you. My son had his demons and it's just unfortunate that he couldn't get the help he needed in time to stop this outcome."

"We are sorry for your loss," Pierce said solemnly.

"I know it's probably too early for you to tell me for sure, but as a professional courtesy, can you please tell me whether or not this was a homicide?" the judge asked.

With all their talking, Jamie hadn't realized until now that they had not actually spoken about what had really happened to Clyde—or actually told the man his son was dead. It was just *known*. The closest thing Pierce had said was in his sympathies. Of course, the judge would have more questions.

"As you know, I can't make any official statements yet, but based on the medical examiner's findings and what we witnessed initially, your son died from a bullet wound to the left temporal lobe."

The judge raised his left hand and pointed his finger at his temple like he was holding a gun. "My son wasn't left-handed, and we are Catholic. We're strong believers that if we committed suicide we would be forever damned to purgatory. I know since his marriage that he hasn't been as devout as he was as a kid, but I know they talked about having children raised in the church as well. I don't see this being a self-inflicted wound."

"We were working off the same assumptions. I didn't know when we arrived today if you were going to be willing to talk to us a little bit more about this situation surrounding his disappearance, and the initial missing persons reports that were filed. If you are, we'd be happy to hear more about what happened and how you found out he had disappeared."

The judge closed his eyes and leaned back in the bench, the wood cracking under his weight as he shifted. The sound echoed around the empty room, almost reminiscent of a small-caliber gunshot.

"I couldn't tell you the exact date when he truly disappeared. However, his wife reported his disappearance on July 24 two years ago. Based on the cell phone records, he had been receiving phone calls. However, one week prior to that, he had made no phone calls and sent no texts. There had also been no financial transactions made with his credit cards during that time frame."

"What did his wife have to say about that?" Pierce asked.

"From the records, I was able to ascertain that she thought he had just ghosted her. They were going through the initial stages of divorce. He had filed, and they were supposed to sit down for a mediation, but he didn't arrive to the meeting. That was when she notified officials, and he was found to be missing."

Jamie had a hard time remaining quiet. Everything in her screamed that Clyde's wife had killed her husband. The timing was just too perfect for her not to have had some role in the man's disappearance. Even if Carey hadn't been the one to pull the trigger, Jamie thought she was behind the man's death. However, she wasn't in a position where she could say a word. Besides, she had a feeling that everyone in this room felt the same way she did. And just as the judge had started their conversation, it was one thing to suspect something to be the truth and another to prove it.

"At that time," the judge continued, "it was the Flathead county sheriff's department that was conducting the search.

They found his cell phone at his home, and so they really had no known last location beyond that which Carey had provided them. I tried to fund a search, and I posted a reward for information leading to his recovery, but nothing ever came from my efforts. I even had billboards, but the only phone calls I ever received were from some teenagers who thought it was funny to call."

"It's hard to perform a search when there's no information. I sympathize with both the sheriff's department and with you and your family. It's a really tough situation." Pierce leaned against the bench and crossed his arms over his chest.

"Yeah, but now I can move on. I'm grateful for that. We have confirmation that he is at least gone. I don't have to question whether he's going to walk in my door. Half of the agony is not knowing. Now our family can grieve and start looking for answers about how this happened and who was behind it." The judge stood up. "I have no doubts that you will do everything in your power to find justice for my son. Whatever resources you need from the county, let me know and I will try to make them happen."

Jamie was absolutely positive that the man was telling the truth, and they could have asked for anything and have gotten it. It wasn't until this moment that she realized how powerful Judge Donovan truly was. In a way, it frightened her.

The judge offered her his hand as they said their goodbyes and he walked them to the doors leading out of the courtroom. There had been many rodeos in which she had felt as though she was out of her league, but she had never felt more out of place than she had during the death notification. Yet she was glad she had witnessed it for Pierce. It helped her understand what he had to go through.

Life and death were so normal. Yet, faced with it like this, it was so visceral and real. It tore at her heart.

She didn't know how Pierce could do that kind of thing every day.

This moment with a father facing his son's loss put her life's tragedy in a new perspective. And while John's death was no less impactful, she was ready to let go of the tragedy as an event and moment in time that would forever define her. She couldn't allow John's death to forge her into someone she didn't quite want to become. She had to let go of what had happened and move on with her life.

Death was a constant and life needed to be lived at its fullest by those death had left behind.

She couldn't fear it and she couldn't keep reliving loss and being stuck in the moment. It would take so much strength, but she had to come back to herself.

If Pierce could find the strength to walk families through these times, she could have the fortitude to walk through it with him by her side.

As they neared Pierce's truck, there was a ping on his cell phone. He helped her up into her seat and then read the text as he walked around to his side of the truck and got in. He was frowning as he threw the device onto the dashboard.

"You did great with the judge in there." She didn't know if she should address the look on his face or just wait for it to disappear naturally.

"Yeah, Judge Donovan was helpful. Definitely backed up what Vince had said and filled in a lot of the holes." Pierce seemed to relax slightly, but his gaze flitted to the phone as he started the truck. "I think we need to make our next stop be the wife's. I have a feeling it may not go nearly as smoothly."

The phone buzzed on the dashboard again, sounding like an angry bee.

"Is everything okay?" she asked, motioning toward the offending device.

He grumbled something under his breath. "It's Reynolds. He wants you and me to come over to his place for dinner tonight to discuss the case. I told him we have too much going on to do a dinner, but he didn't budge." He grabbed the phone and shoved it into the cupholder in the console between the seats by the computer.

"Why wouldn't he just meet you at headquarters?"

"To be honest, I think he needs his wife's care in the evenings. After his car accident, he had the option to retire, but he came back while he was still recovering, and he's been doing a great job. Sometimes, though, we have to move around protocols and normal procedures to make sure he gets what he needs to be cared for appropriately. That's way more important than policies, but in this case… I'd rather be questioning people and sending him an email or jumping on the phone."

"How did his accident happen?" Jamie asked.

"It happened early in the fall a couple of years ago. He was just leaving the park—and he doesn't remember what happened. But, from the accident report and the recreated scene, Highway Patrol assumed that he must have swerved to avoid hitting an animal or something in the road and he ended up rolling his vehicle. He was thrown through the windshield. There is major injury to the C4, 5 and 6 as well as lower in his vertebral column. I saw the X-ray once of his back, and it looked like an S when they brought him into the ER." He gave her a wide-eyed expression.

"It sounds like he is incredibly lucky he even survived. How did he not have a major TBI? Was he a different man—you know, *cognitively*—after the accident?"

Pierce nodded. "Yes and no. I don't think that he had a TBI, surprisingly. It must have been how he hit, but most of the impact was his back and spine. They found him at the base of a tree, so there's some conjecture that he actually hit the tree, which might have saved him from dying instantly. Who knows?"

Pierce pulled out onto the road.

They made their way back through the center of downtown Kalispell and toward the older residential side of the town leading north.

"One thing is certain," Pierce continued, "he had a new perspective on life, and he poured himself into work as soon as he was out of the hospital."

That surprised her. If she had been in his situation and could not have gone back to work and spent her life behind a desk, she would have chosen to spend the rest of her days experiencing all the things life had to offer. She would travel the world and see all the horse arenas she had yet to visit. Then again, she assumed it had to be hard for Reynolds to travel. Her grandfather had been in a wheelchair for the last five years of his life, and though many things had been adapted to make life easier for those who needed mobility aids, there was still a long way to go to making things truly manageable—even airplanes.

"I bet his wife is glad he survived. And I'm sure he's grateful that she is there by his side. Do you think that's why he chose to stay here and just devote himself to Glacier?"

"I don't know what it is about this town, but before the accident, there was talk that Reynolds and his wife were on the rocks. If anything, I think that it saved their marriage. The things that they both had to learn to rely on each other."

She was surprised. "I thought when things like that happened, it tore people apart, I didn't realize that it could go the other way. That actually kind of helps restore my faith in humanity."

He chuckled, turning down a road in front of one of the local high schools. The place was deserted, except for a black sweatshirt that was hanging on the fence, forgotten by a child. There was something deeply sad about it.

"I don't know much about their relationship now, but Reynolds tries to be in control of things at the office. I don't always agree with his decisions, but I think that's the nature of a boss." He laughed.

A block ahead of them, a blacked-out Suburban was parked on the side of the road. She recognized it as Emily's work vehicle. She must have been waiting for them— or, rather, Pierce.

She glanced over at Pierce. He was staring at the house at the end of the cul-de-sac. It was a millennial-gray house, with two fake cedar trees in gray plastic barrels at the end of the driveway. It had white windows and white doors with thin black accents, and it looked like every other house on the block. It almost looked like it had been cut out of any advertisement for any construction company in any state in America.

It was a nice house; it just wasn't anything special. From

what she had learned about Donovan's wife, gossip queen who was likely a Black Widow, the blandness seemed to fit.

It struck her how she had never met this woman, and only knew her through reputation and what she had learned in passing, and yet she already despised her. That was almost a gift, for someone to leave that kind of social trail.

Jamie tried to tell herself that she needed to give the woman a fair shot, but the evil part of her chuckled exactly where she wanted to place the shot. Her father would have said center mass, or two to the chest and one to the head.

Yeah, that wasn't going to help the situation.

"When we get up here, I think it's best if you stay in the truck while I question Carey." Pierce motioned toward the witch's gingerbread house.

"I think that's fair. I'll be here when you get back." She held back the desire to mention the fact that he probably shouldn't leave behind a gun.

After spending the morning with Clyde's father and seeing the pain in his eyes, this woman was just lucky Jamie didn't believe in vigilante justice.

Chapter Sixteen

Pierce was looking forward to this death notification just about as much as he would have looked forward to jumping into a pit of rattlesnakes. He had met Carey Donovan once before at a Mule Deer Foundation banquet she had been at with Clyde.

She'd been wearing a skintight leopard-print dress that was two sizes too small on her large frame. She had to have been at least six feet tall, but probably more. Her boobs had been the talk of the night, as they had been precariously close to absolutely falling out of the top of the dress.

She had been hanging on to an investment banker out of California all night; the guy had been bidding on a private hunt on a ten-thousand-acre ranch in eastern Montana. If he remembered correctly, the guy had ended up walking away with the prize for close to forty thousand dollars. He couldn't imagine paying that kind of money for a stinky mule deer, no matter how big it was. The word around the bar later had been that the out-of-stater had also walked out with her. Something told Pierce he hadn't had to pay quite as much for that leopard-print dress to hit the floor.

He parked behind Emily and walked up to her window, leaving Jamie behind in his truck. Jamie had seemed only too happy to wait. He couldn't blame her. There was not a single part of him that wanted to do this, either.

He tapped on Emily's window and it slowly rolled down.

"How's it going?" he asked as Emily came into view.

She shrugged. "I've had better days, but it is what it is. I've seen some motion in the house, so I think that our girl is home. Given what we know about her, I think it may be better if you're the one to do the talking, she may respond better to a male."

He wasn't sure if he actually agreed with that logic, but he could understand Emily's line of thinking. "Well, let's get this over with. Do you know what you want to ask her? This may be our only shot before she lawyers up."

"Knowing this woman, she might have that done before we even make it to the door."

Pierce chuckled as he opened Emily's door for her and waited for her to step out. "Let's just see how this goes."

There wasn't even the sound of birds as they made their way up to the front door. It was almost like there was a calm before the storm.

He tried to find some thread of hope within himself that he was wrong in his assumptions about how this would all go. Then again, it was better to plan for the worst than hope for the best.

There was a camera doorbell and he pushed the button. A woman's voice came over the speaker. "Can I help you?" Her voice was shrill and flecked with a Valley Girl accent.

Emily stepped closer. "Hi, I'm Detective Monahan with the Flathead County Sheriff's Office. I was hoping to talk to you today. Can you please step outside?"

The woman gave an audible groan, as if they were interrupting her day. "I'm working. Can this wait?"

What kind of person told a police officer on their front porch to come back later, when it was more convenient for them?

Pierce could feel annoyance start to simmer in his belly. He normally wasn't an angry man, but this woman put him on edge. In an effort to control his temper, he clenched his jaw.

"Mrs. Donovan, this will not wait. You need to come to the door and speak with us. I'm sure your boss will understand."

There was a long pause, like the woman was trying to decide whether she would do as she was told or if she would continue to press her luck. While they had no probable cause to file for a search warrant yet, if she kept up this kind of behavior, it wouldn't take much to compile enough evidence to get the laws on their side—and it would stand up in court.

"I'll be down in five minutes. I need to put on my makeup."

Of course she did.

"We will be here," Emily said, sounding as annoyed as he felt.

There was an audible click on the other end of the line.

He leaned against the house and crossed his arms over his chest beside Emily as they waited. Emily was working away on her phone, but he couldn't see what she was working on. Jamie waved at him from the truck, and he gave her an acknowledging tip of the head to let her know everything was going to be okay.

Jamie glanced away and he took the chance to really look at her and the way the sun streamed through the windshield and caught the gold in her hair. Her locks lay loose around her shoulders, and she was running her fingers lazily through the strands. She closed her eyes, smiling and tilting her face up into the rays. She was so beautiful.

The front door of the house burst open. The tall woman stood there in too small jeans and a sage-colored crop top. She had eyelashes glued on that were so long and cheap-looking that they almost looked like black moths stuck on her eyelids. "What do you want?"

Emily stepped forward and put her foot just inside the door frame so the woman couldn't close the door. "Do you mind if we step inside so we can talk, Mrs. Donovan?"

The woman scowled. "Fine. Whatever." She motioned toward the small living room. It was painted pale gray and had two matching linen-gray couches at its center and a television mounted on the wall above a white fireplace. On the wall, near the front window, was a *Live Laugh Love* sign like Haven used to have.

She walked in, flopped down on the couch and motioned for them to sit opposite. "So, are you guys going to tell me what was so urgent, or are you gonna just waste my time all day?"

Everything about Carey was abrasive. He couldn't understand how she had ever even gotten married in the first place. There had to be some attribute of her that was positive. He looked at her face, trying to ignore the sneer on her lips. In the conventional sense, she was pretty with her dark brunette hair and green eyes.

Even when a woman was good-looking, with a personality like hers, it didn't matter. Ugly was ugly. It was the soul that made a woman beautiful.

Maybe Clyde just had the same ugly soul. Pierce and the former mayor had never really spent much time together, but what little they had, they hadn't clicked. Clyde was the kind of guy who landed somewhere in the gray area when it came to legal matters. And there were always rumblings about his willingness to get his business dealings handled.

In fact, an entire strip mall had been purchased and turned into housing for the homeless because of Clyde. In theory, it was commendable, and philanthropic. However, it was later found out that Clyde had ended up making three million dollars on the deal thanks to the suppliers who'd not only remodeled the shopping center but also from the companies that had supplied the warming shelter with everything it needed.

He was definitely a man who could have been bought. And with that, it made him think of Carey's leopard dress. Maybe that was exactly what had brought these two people together into marriage.

If Clyde's wife hadn't killed him, there would be a long list of people who could have also been suspects. They could potentially spend years looking into the nefarious deeds of this man. However, Pierce had a feeling that Judge Donovan was never going to agree that was what had happened. If they didn't find answers and the person behind this, not only would the judge start to handle this himself, but Pierce and Emily would probably be out of jobs. The judge was a shark.

Emily cleared her throat. "As I stated outside, I am Detective Emily Monahan, and this is my colleague, Ranger Pierce Hauser. We are here today to let you know that we found your husband's remains. And he is deceased."

Carey's face didn't move. She didn't even blink. "Where did you find him?"

It struck him how this woman was the only person they

had run into all day who had not heard about their findings. In this small town, there was no way someone hadn't already called her.

Perhaps that was why there was such a lack of emotive response. That, or she really was *that* cold. Even though they were going through a divorce, he would have thought there would have been some kind of sadness or even relief to know for sure what had happened to Clyde.

Then again, if she had something to do with his disappearance and death, this is exactly the kind of response he would expect.

"We located him high up on a mountain near Avalanche Lake, in the park." Emily tented her fingers between her knees. "It does appear as though he died from a gunshot wound, and at this point we are looking for the weapon used. Do you know if your husband owned any guns?"

Carey frowned, and he noticed the deep wrinkles between her eyes. "First of all, he and I were on the outs. I'm sure you guys know that already if you were standing at my door. It wasn't a secret. And I also want to make it clear that I didn't have anything to do with his disappearance. I've already been down this road. Everyone wanted to question me when he first went missing and I'm tired of that crap."

Emily sat back on the couch, like she was trying to stay out of the line of fire.

"I'm sure that you've been through the ringer with your husband's disappearance." Pierce took the reins. "We don't think that you had anything to do with this," he lied. "We just are trying to accumulate as much information as we can to bring closure to his family and to you."

"Listen, I'm glad you found him. Seriously, I think that's great. But my closure came the day I went down to the courthouse and filed the paperwork to have him declared dead. If I could have done that the day he filed for divorce, that would have been even better."

Whew. She definitely hated the man, but there was something in the way she spoke that made him actually question whether or not she was the one who'd murdered him.

It was like she wouldn't have been as angry if she had been the one behind it. Pierce would imagine that perhaps he would have been more sedate and less toxic.

It was a strange logic, but he just had a feeling.

"Do you know anyone who would have wanted your husband dead?" he asked.

She rubbed her finger at the corner of her eye, smearing some of her black eyeliner. "You could start with any of the number of women he was sleeping with. Maybe one of them found out about the other, that's what I told the police when he first went missing. You can look up their names in one of the police reports. I don't know if the numbers are still accurate for their phones but have at it." She waved him off.

"I'm assuming since the police did not make any headway on that," he said, looking over at Emily who almost imperceptibly shook her head. "That your theory about his mistresses or girlfriends didn't pan out. Do you have any other ideas about people who would want him dead? Business partners? Colleagues?"

She glared at him like he had stepped out of line by going against her in any way about Donovan's mistresses. "I hardly ever knew what he was doing at work. He was always at dinner with someone. Usually it was with women, and I don't know if those were actually work dinners or 'working dinners.'" She made quotation marks with her fingers. "I finally had enough of him. I told him no more women. I said if I caught him with any more that we were done."

"So, you caught him with a woman?" Emily asked.

"One of my friends saw him walking into a hotel with a woman who worked for the US Marshals' office. She sent me pictures of them walking inside and standing at the lobby desk. She waited, and then she sent me pictures of them leaving a few hours later." There was a flatness in her voice that told him she had retold this story many times, to the point that she had become desensitized.

"That's a good friend." Emily nodded.

The woman shrugged.

"Why didn't you just leave him at that point?" Pierce asked.

"I loved him. I thought I could forgive him." Carey stared out the front windows as though she wished she could use them as some form of escape. "I have thought a lot after he first went missing about what could have happened to him. That initial period of time, I really thought he had just holed up with some woman and he was being a jerk and playing some stupid legal game with me that I didn't understand. I'd never been through a divorce before. He had, so I didn't know."

Emily leaned forward and she touched the woman's knee. She must have been feeling something for this woman's plight as well. When they had gotten here, he had never in a million years thought he would have left questioning his assumptions about this woman.

"The only thing I can come up with that I didn't discuss with the police when he initially disappeared was a business deal he was working on with the park. I don't know much about it. I just remember hearing him talking about a merchandising option with the city and the park, and money exchanging hands." She shrugged.

Pierce leaned back on the couch. A branding deal with the park would have included their marketing team, and he didn't know a ton of people in that department. He'd have to ask around, but it was worth looking into. Just like everything else with this case, it seemed far-fetched and a probable dead end.

"That's super helpful, thank you," Pierce said. "You said that you were willing to forgive your husband for his problematic behavior, but then he went ahead and filed for divorce. Is that correct?"

She nodded.

"That strikes me as unusual. Normally, in these situations, at least by what I know about national averages, women are the ones who initiate these types of divorces. Why was he the one to file? And how long after the fact, and you finding out, did this filing take place?"

"It was probably six months, maybe more. I don't have a head for dates. We'd had a pretty nasty fight—he told me he never wanted to see me again. He just picked up and left."

"What was this fight about?" Emily asked.

The woman moved away from Emily's hand and her body closed off. "I don't recall."

She was lying. Her body language and her words didn't align. What she had just said had been well-coached by a lawyer.

Carey stood. "I need to get back to work. I appreciate you letting me know about Clyde. As for his death, I've given you everything I know. If you have any other questions, I'm working with the DB Law Group. You can contact me through them." She motioned toward the door.

As Pierce stood to leave, the empathy he had been feeling for this woman slipped away. He wasn't sure if she was innocent or just a really good liar who excelled at playing the victim.

Chapter Seventeen

Jamie watched as Emily and Pierce walked together toward the pickup. Their heads were low and they were deep in conversation. She couldn't tell from the looks on their faces how the meeting had gone, but it had taken much longer than she had anticipated.

When they had arrived at the cul-de-sac, she wasn't even sure that they would go into the house. In the end, they had spent more time with this woman than they had with the judge. It made her wonder how much the woman had told them. Now, she wished she had gone inside, but it really hadn't been her place, and it would have been awkward.

She rolled down the window as they neared. "How'd it go?"

Pierce looked at her and she could see the confusion in his face. He looked more lost than when he had walked in. *Interesting.*

"She had a lot to talk about," Emily said. "In the end, she ended up lawyering up."

"Isn't that a sure sign that somebody's guilty?" she asked, looking at Pierce for some unspoken tell.

"In this case, I really don't know if she is or isn't, and we are going to have a hard time proving it if she is. I don't know if she's really smart or just a really good liar," Pierce said.

Emily nodded. "I have the same feeling. I don't know if she's guilty or not. But she's definitely made a life of getting what she wants regardless of who she hurts."

She seemed to be guilty of something, even if it wasn't the crime they were there to investigate. She might deserve to go to jail, but time would tell how things would play out. If she had played a role in Clyde's murder, and if she knew that she was being investigated, it wouldn't surprise her if this woman ran. They needed to find answers, and now Jamie hoped they would get them before this woman disappeared.

Pierce looked down at his watch. "Hey, we need to get running. My patrol captain was chomping at the bit to get an update on the case. I'm sure your captain is as well."

Emily nodded. "Given the family name, you know my captain's on my ass. I wouldn't be surprised if Judge Donovan has already talked to him. I'm sure I'll be sitting at his desk in the morning, being dressed down about how I need to work faster and find out exactly who was the one pulling the trigger."

"I have a feeling both of our necks are on the chopping block. There's a lot at stake." Pierce sighed.

"Let's plan on meeting up again in the morning and hitting it hard. We'll come up with a game plan and go from there. I'll send you over all the investigation reports into Clyde's initial disappearance. You can study up tonight," she said, her gaze slipping to Jamie. "That is, if you're not too busy." She sent her a little devious smirk.

Jamie felt the heat rise in her cheeks. She quickly looked away.

"I will be studying," he said, checking Emily's little attempt at humor.

"Oh, you guys are no fun," Emily said. "You two make a cute couple and there's nothing wrong with you spending the night together." She winked at Jamie. "We won't expect you back at the ranch tonight—have fun." She turned and waved as she hurried off. She didn't give her the option for a ride home.

Jamie was glad.

She wasn't sure she was ready to jump into bed with Pierce, but she was ready to spend more time with him, even if that meant sitting around with him while he read police reports. "If I'll be in the way, you can run me back. Or I can get a ride," she offered.

Emily got into her Suburban and waved as she passed by. Jamie stuck out her tongue. Pierce laughed. "Don't worry about being in the way. I want you around. Besides, my boss and his wife are expecting us for dinner. I would hate to have to tell them you stood them up. It would be horrible for my reputation."

"Oh, your reputation? Is that what you care about?" she teased, playfully ignoring the bit where he had admitted he had wanted her around.

He tilted his back with a laugh as he made his way around and got into the truck.

As they hit the road, he slipped his hand into hers, and it felt so natural as he told her about their interview with Carey that she almost didn't hear what he was talking about. Yet, it was so interesting—the duality of the woman, the victim and the antagonist.

In some ways, it felt like the duality of this moment, her hand in his. Hers callused by leather reins and bailing twine. His softened by time behind steering wheels and telephones. Yet, he was arguably the stronger and tougher between them.

It was striking how quickly life, feelings and the world could change.

As they arrived at the cabin on the outskirts of West Glacier, tucked back into the mountains, she was taken by the quaint charm of the place. It looked like something out of a Thomas Kinkade painting her parents used to have. Complete with the cabin's wraparound porch and a chimney with white smoke pouring out into the dusky summer sky.

As they stepped out of the truck, the air smelled of barbecued meats and baked potatoes, and her mouth watered. It had been hours since they'd had breakfast at the greasy spoon and though it had been that morning, it didn't even feel as if it had been the same day. So much had happened, it felt as though had been weeks ago.

There was a small ramp up to the porch and her boots thumped on the plywood as they made their way to the door. It opened before they even had a chance to knock. "Hey, guys," a brunette woman said, giving them a thin-lipped smile.

The woman was beautiful, curvy, and had sparkling brown eyes. "Come in, come in. We have been waiting for you," she said, excitedly, waving them inside.

The house was sparsely decorated and the leather furniture that was there was kept wide apart so Eliot's wheelchair could maneuver more easily through the space. There was a table off to one side that held a collection of medical devices, items to help the man breathe, including what she recognized as a nebulizer.

Though Jamie had realized the man had significant

health problems, she hadn't known how much of his body had been impacted by his paralysis. It did make sense his lungs would have issues. It made her wonder how he continued to work, but she was impressed.

"Thank you so much for having us in your beautiful home," Jamie said, motioning toward the fireplace where they had a small fire going. "I love how you've done everything. I've always wanted a rock fireplace."

"I know it's summer and it seems silly to have fire, but it still gets a little chilly up here at night. Plus, I just think it's fun to have a fire for guests. You know?" The woman smiled brightly at the compliment as she glanced at the warm flames. "Thank you. And, oh, by the way, you can call me Nicole. I'm Eliot's wife. He's outside watching the barbecue for me while I was getting the door. I heard you guys coming up the road. You know how it is out here in the timber—you can hear people coming from a mile away." She laughed.

From the chipper way the woman spoke and from her drawl, Jamie guessed she was from somewhere down south, maybe Mississippi. She seemed like a nice woman, if a little too chatty—but perhaps it was just nerves at having strangers coming into her home.

"It's nice to meet you, Nicole. I've heard really great things about you."

She waved her off as she looked demurely away. "Oh, come now. It's all lies."

Pierce didn't argue with her, and it made Jamie wonder. Most people she knew would have politely bantered with the woman—especially given the fact it was his boss's wife.

"I'm going to head out to the grill," Pierce said, motioning outside. "Mind if I grab a beer?"

Nicole shook her head. "Wait, let me grab you a cold one. You don't need to serve yourself here. You're our guest."

She hurried into the kitchen, which was attached to the living room in an open-concept design, and grabbed two beers from the fridge. She opened the drawer with the clatter of silverware and rummaged around until she pulled out a bottle opener and clumsily flipped off the lids, letting one fall to the floor.

Her hands were shaking slightly as she handed the first brown bottle over to Pierce. "There you are. Tell Eliot I'll get him some water when he comes in."

Pierce lifted the bottle in thanks. "You got it." He turned on his heel and made his way outside.

Jamie hadn't really seen Pierce be this curt before and she was slightly taken aback. She would have thought this was Pierce in a professional setting, but this wasn't even the same Pierce she had seen in Eliot's office—just here, with Nicole. It was almost as if she made Pierce uncomfortable.

As he stepped outside and closed the door behind him, some of the tension seemed to leave with him. Nicole sighed as she reached over and handed her the other bottle of beer before grabbing one out of the fridge and opening another for herself. "He *really* doesn't like me," Nicole said, just confronting the elephant in the room and surprising Jamie.

"I don't think it's that. Pierce hasn't said anything to that effect about you to me." She tried to take some of the sting out of the woman's assumption, even if Jamie wondered the same.

"I don't know why, but he has never really warmed up to me. Tonight, though, he seems really *off*. Maybe you're right, it's probably just to do with this case with the former mayor. I heard it was a homicide investigation now."

The woman knew more than Jamie had expected, but then she was a patrol captain's wife. It made sense that he would take his work home and talk to her about his day.

"It is. Gunshot wound. I don't think they've found the gun."

"David and Vince are up there with the dogs. If it's there, they will find it. Those guys are great. Vince is a good ranger. Very *thorough*."

"I met him this morning. He seems like a good guy."

"Who did you meet?"

"Vince."

"Oh, yeah." Nicole smiled as she picked at the edge of the paper label on her beer bottle before taking a sip. "He is. He was supposed to be in Pierce's wedding party. Did you know that?" Nicole jerked her head up. "Oh, did Pierce even tell you about that?" She motioned toward her, awkwardly, and squished her face.

"He did tell me about it, yes."

"That was a sad deal. She was horrible to him. Damaged the whole family. I think he may still love her, though." She glanced at Jamie like she was goading her for a response.

She still didn't really want to discuss Pierce or his wedding with this woman—especially if there was some reason for tension between her and Pierce. If Nicole was one for gossip and drama, that could have been exactly what the problem was and why Pierce had high-tailed it outside.

In fact, she was going to give him a piece of her mind for leaving her as the fall guy with this woman when they were alone again. And, if he still loved his ex, which she was darned near sure he didn't, she would be giving him a whole lot more than a piece of her mind.

"What do you do for work?" Jamie asked, trying to gently change the subject.

Nicole leaned against the counter. "I used to be a certified nurse's assistant at Logan's, but when Eliot got hurt, I decided to stay home and become his full-time health-care provider. Social security pays me a salary, and it's actually more than I was making before at the hospital, so it works out great."

If she wasn't mistaken, it sounded like Nicole was almost grateful her husband had gotten hurt. There was no wonder Pierce didn't like her.

"That's nice that you can and are willing to provide him with the care he needs, but he seems pretty independent and capable in his daily life."

Nicole scowled, like Jamie had somehow offended *her* by questioning the validity of her taking on a full-time role when Eliot clearly didn't need it. "He needs a lot more help than most people realize."

Jamie put her hands up in submission. "I'm sorry, you are absolutely right. I'd had a grandfather who spent the last few years of his life with limited mobility, and he relied on a wheelchair to get around. I know it can be a challenge."

"That's not the same as a man being paralyzed."

"Again," Jamie said, dropping her head in apology, "you're correct. I'm sorry. I'm just trying to relate with your life and what you must be going through, but I know I have no real idea of what it must be like for you. I'd be happy to listen if you want to tell me about it, though." She felt like such a jerk, but she had been well intended.

"Eliot cannot take care of his personal hygiene adequately. So, several times a day, I have to move him from his wheelchair, with the help of a lift and make sure he is clean and dry. Often, he has sores because of his position in the chair. Because he can't feel the sores, they can quickly get out of control if we don't pay attention." Nicole let it all pour out, as if she had been waiting for someone to let her just vent. "And that is to say nothing about when he runs his legs into things—he has broken his foot twice and he had no idea until I took his shoe off and his foot was black and blue."

"It has to be so hard to be a personal caregiver."

"It is. And it is taxing. I love him, but he isn't the same since his accident. It's like I'm married to a man I don't even know." She picked at the label until a piece tore off. "I feel more like a nurse than I do a wife, but he wants me as both. It can be *hard*."

She had not liked the woman, but as Nicole opened up to her and poured her heart out to her, Jamie found herself warming to the woman. Clearly, she didn't have anyone to talk to and she just needed to have a safe space to let out her thoughts and feelings. Tonight, that could be her.

Jamie was grateful that when she'd been going through her darkest days, she'd had Matt by her side. He'd been there to talk to about all her memories and then how they were going to move through the future. Sometimes it had been hard to even move from day to day with his help. She couldn't imagine what it was like for Nicole—and it wasn't like she could talk to her husband.

"You should come out to the ranch. I was thinking about starting a riding clinic or equine therapy or something. It could be something to get you out of the house while Eliot's at work and it could be something you do just for yourself. I mean if you are interested in something like that?"

Nicole smiled, and for the first time Jamie noticed her

right canine tooth had a large chip in it that made it appear almost straight. "That would be great. I had been seeing a therapist for a while, but that didn't work out. I went to a few, but none of them really helped and I just decided to stop. Maybe therapy with animals would be better."

"Do whatever helps. In order to help others, you must take care of yourself. You know, that whole *put your own oxygen mask on first* thing." Jamie took a sip from her beer.

"Did I tell you I ran into one of your ranch hands the other day in town?" Nicole asked, tilting her head like a confused dog.

"Oh really? Do you know who it was?"

There was the creak of the back door as it swung open and there was the whirr of the electric wheelchair as Eliot rolled inside. "Hey, Jamie, how's it going?" he asked, moving the chair forward with the black knob in his hand.

"It's going, Eliot. Thanks for inviting me over for dinner. It's appreciated." She sent Nicole a grateful smile. "Ranch food is great, but when you raise beef, it's steak every night for dinner."

Nicole laughed. "Well, you're in luck, tonight we made brats." As she spoke, Pierce walked in through the back door carrying a tray of blackened brats and toasted buns.

They looked delicious and her mouth started to water.

"Do you need me to do anything?" Jamie asked, motioning toward the cupboards. "I can set the table or whatever you need."

Nicole nodded. "Step over here and I'll hand you the plates. We will just load up here in the kitchen and make our way over to the table." She pointed in the direction of the adjoining dining room where there was a large log table, sans one chair where Eliot must put his wheelchair. "Pierce, you can put that tray down on the stove there."

They all moved through the kitchen like a well-orchestrated dance thanks to the maven's commands. Eliot moved toward the dining room. "I'll have one brat," he called back to Nicole. "And a baked potato. No salad."

Nicole rolled her eyes at the order. "You can say 'please,' Eliot." There was a noticeable chill in her tone.

Eliot huffed. "Please. Thank you. Whatever."

Nicole opened the microwave and pulled out a plate of steaming potatoes crusted in salt. She placed them on the stove next to the tray and then she grabbed the plates out of the cupboard and handed them to Jamie. "Can you put these over there," she said, pointing to a space on the counter. "I'll grab the salad that Eliot will most definitely be having." She looked back at her husband with annoyance.

Pierce sent Jamie a look, like he wanted to know if she could feel the thick animosity between the couple as much as he could. She lifted one shoulder. After what Nicole revealed to her, she could understand some of the woman's frustrations with her marriage. She was in a hard place. Now, Jamie wished she'd had a chance to ask her if she still loved him. If Nicole didn't, it would make it even harder to watch.

Maybe this was why they didn't have a lot of dinner guests.

She would just have to eat fast.

Nicole placed the bowl of salad beside the potatoes and moved to grab the condiments for everything from the fridge. Jamie turned to the silverware drawer and pulled out what they would need, to speed things up.

Grabbing a plate, she dished up food and handed it over to Pierce. "Here you go."

Nicole turned with a bottle of ketchup in her hand and looked at his plate with the bratwurst with a tilt of the head. "Um, do you need this?" she asked, offering him the bottle.

He shook his head. "Nah, I'm good." He glanced at Jamie and smiled.

He must have read her mind about wanting to get out of this place.

"Can I get Eliot's plate together for you?" Jamie asked, grabbing the next white plate in the stack.

"No, that's fine," Nicole said, taking the plate and starting to put things together. She sliced up the bratwurst and put the ketchup and mustard on the side of the plate for him to dip. She dropped some Caesar salad on the side and a mashed up baked potato, topped with butter and salt and pepper.

As she worked, Jamie prepared a light plate. She was hungry, but she made herself a simple brat and salad so she could plow through. She moved to the table and sat down next to Pierce. He touched his elbow to hers; a simple gesture but one that was greatly appreciated.

Nicole placed the plate on the table in front of Eliot along with a larger gripped fork. His arm trembled as he picked up the fork and stabbed it into the first piece of meat and dipped it into the ketchup. "So, David called tonight and said that they have a hit on the location the guy died. The anthropologists came in and started the dig. We are going to have the results back from that tonight, hopefully." Eliot looked at their plates. "Go ahead and start eating, you don't need to wait for her."

Pierce cleared his throat and gave a nervous laugh. "No,

that's okay. She cooked, we don't want to offend our host." He sent Nicole a smile as she came walking over to the table with a plate.

Nicole slipped into the chair one away from her husband after setting down a glass of water for him by his plate. "Thanks, Pierce. Really, you guys can dig in. We want you fed. You've been working hard."

Pierce picked up his fork. "It sounds like the park team is the one who has been working the hardest."

Eliot's phone pinged but he glanced down at it and ignored it. Instead, he chewed his bite for a long time before swallowing. He took a scoop of potatoes, but carefully avoided the salad. "How did the notifications go? How did Judge Donovan take the news?"

"You didn't get a phone call?" Pierce asked, sounding surprised.

"You know I did. I think every high-ranking official involved with this case got a phone call. He did tell me he was impressed with you. I don't know what you said, or did in there, but good job." Eliot lowered his arm, letting it relax on the table. "That being said, he also made it clear you have by the end of the week to wrap this up, or I'm to make sure you are no longer working at Glacier National Park."

"He doesn't have the right to do that," Pierce countered, anger in his voice.

"I said the same thing, though slightly more tactfully." Eliot let out a long exhale. "He and I had a long talk. There were many threats—to both of us. You just need to get this handled. Quickly."

Eliot's phone pinged again.

Pierce's phone buzzed in his back pocket.

"You guys probably need to answer that," Nicole said,

motioning toward Eliot's phone. "We all know when you guys get calls at the same time, it spells trouble."

Pierce pulled out his phone and answered. "Hello?"

Jamie looked at his face. At first, it was pinched with anger from the conversation with Eliot, but as the person on the other end of the line spoke, his gaze moved to her and his eyes widened, and she could see the color drain from his cheeks.

"What happened? What's wrong?" she asked, suddenly very afraid.

She tried to think of anything that would make him look at *her* like that. She wasn't involved with anything that was happening, she had just been helping with the case. What had she done?

Pierce nodded. "I got it, I'll be right there. Thanks for calling me." He clicked off the phone and stood up from the table. "Eliot, Nicole, we have to go. I'm sorry. Thank you for dinner." He held out his hand and Jamie put her shaking hand in his as he helped her to stand.

"What's going on?"

He shook his head as he looked at her. "I'll tell you outside in the truck. We have to go. Now."

She nodded as she let him lead her from the table. As they neared the front door, she remembered what she had been doing. "Yes," she said, looking back over her shoulder at their hosts, "thank you for dinner."

"Any time," Nicole called after her as they walked out the door and clicked it shut behind them.

Pierce didn't let go of her hand as he pulled her toward the truck and helped her inside. He gave her hand one last clutch before letting go and closing her door.

He got in, put the truck in gear and hit the gas, hard. He

kicked out dirt and gravel as they sped off down the dirt road and back toward the highway.

"Are you going to tell me what is going on or keep me guessing, Mario Andretti?"

He exhaled and the action made her stomach clench with nerves. "Something's happened to Matt."

She felt like she had gotten punched right in the gut. "What? What *happened*?"

"A man found him down outside The Mint Bar in town. Someone got their hands on him and beat him pretty bad. He is in the hospital. They have him intubated. He's in a medically-induced coma, and not doing well."

She had been so wrapped up in Pierce and what they were doing that she had barely been thinking about Matt. He was her best friend, and she had just left him to do his thing for the last couple of days. What kind of friend was she when he had come up here for her to help at her family's ranch and make sure she was settled?

Her thoughts moved to Eliot and Nicole. She would have to call Sally in Juneau and have her come down to see her husband. Sally was not going to take the news well. She had been freaking out over the cat attack, and now this. She was going to be a mess.

Once again, it struck her how quickly things could change and how, in this moment, Sally was going to do as she had once done—she was going to rush to a man who was on the brink of death. Hopefully, she would make it in time.

Chapter Eighteen

When they arrived at the hospital, the staff turned them away as it was after visiting hours. Pierce had tried to argue their way in, telling them about the situation and flashing his badge, but they'd made no special concessions as they weren't immediate family. He felt as though he had failed Jamie.

He looked out the window toward the parking lot, where she was standing beside the truck, talking on the phone. Tears were running down her cheeks and she was rubbing them away with the back of her free hand as she spoke.

She had told him she was calling Matt's wife, Sally. He'd offered to make the call for her, and watching her in this pain, he wished she had taken him up on his offer. It killed him to see her crying; his entire body yearned to go to her and do anything to staunch her agony.

There was so little he could do to help, but he could at least see what the local police were doing to find the person who had done this to Jamie's best friend. He pulled out his phone and called Emily. She answered on the first ring. "Hello?"

"Did you hear about Matt Goldstock? You know, the attack at The Mint?" he asked, not bothering with niceties.

Emily shuffled the phone, and it sounded like she must

have been in bed. "Yeah, I saw the call-out, but I don't know anything about it." She sounded tired.

"Matt is the guy who was on the trail with Jamie. I don't have proof, but I think this attack might have something to do with our case."

There was a pause and the ruffle of linens. "Why would you say that?" she asked, sounding more alert.

"Matt didn't have any enemies here. Jamie said he isn't the kind to run his mouth and cause problems." He ran his hand over his face. "I know this guy's attack isn't your call, but I'd appreciate you getting involved and looking into it. You need to look through the lens of our investigation. Who has ties to our guy?"

He could hear Emily getting out of bed and her footfalls. "I'll get on it."

"Hey, I'm sorry if I woke you up."

"It's part and parcel of the whole genie gig." She exhaled a thin, tired laugh. "Where are you guys right now? Are you safe?"

"We are," he said, worriedly glancing out the window at Jamie. He hadn't wanted to think about what Matt's attack could have meant about their own safety, but the potential for their being attacked next had been moving through the back of his mind. "We're at the hospital right now. I was hoping she could get in to see Matt. He's in the ICU, but they're not letting us in. Honestly, it's probably not a bad thing. He's in pretty bad shape, according to what I heard from my friends at Dispatch."

"Is he going to make it through the night?"

He rubbed his face as he leaned back against the white hospital wall. That was something else he had tried to avoid thinking about. "I'm hoping so. The hospital staff won't release any information to us because we aren't family. Jamie is on the phone with the guy's wife now. Maybe she can get more out of them."

"You know, if they're not letting you in… It's probably a good thing they are sticking to visiting hours in the ICU. A lot of time, they will bypass those kinds of rules for people who are actively dying."

It wasn't great, but it was at least something he could give Jamie to make the night go by a little easier until they could see Matt in the morning.

"Let me know if you get any more information on the beating."

"I'm sure we can pull footage from around the bar, they have cameras up all over around that place, for obvious reasons." Emily exhaled, like she was pulling on a shoe. "I'll call you when I get something." She hung up the phone.

He appreciated that she wasn't messing around, but it probably expedited the process thanks to the fact that Matt was an employee at her and her husband's ranch.

He walked through the automatic door that led outside just as Jamie was hanging up. Her eyes were puffy, and she rubbed the bottom of her palms against them to try to control herself. "He's going to be okay."

"Did you talk to one of his doctors? Did they tell you something?" she asked, sounding hopeful.

"No," he said, taking her by the hand and trying to comfort her, "but I spoke to Emily, and she reminded me that if staff is under the impression a person is on the verge of death, they often let friends into the room to say goodbye. They don't want anyone to have to be alone or without those they love. So, they must be confident he is stable enough that he will make it through the night."

She sniffled and tilted her head back, shaking out her hands. "Good, that's good. I'll tell Sally that. She'll like it. It will make her feel less stressed while she makes her way here."

"So, she is on her way?"

Jamie nodded.

At least he knew Matt would be in good hands if his wife was going to come in from Alaska. He hated hospital policies sometimes, especially in cases like these where no one from the family was near. It wasn't the same to simply talk to a doctor or nurse on the phone instead of standing with your loved ones while they received hands-on care.

THEY WERE JUST about to the ranch when Jamie turned to him. "Can we go back to your house? I don't want to be here tonight." She motioned to the rusted metal sign with their brand, which listed gently in the moonlight from where it hung on the log over the driveway.

"As you wish, you know you are always welcome. I'm glad you want to," he said, laying his hand on the console between them and putting his palm up.

She slipped her hand into his.

"I just don't want to sleep alone tonight if there is someone out there who is upset we're looking into Donovan's murder. I'm tough, but I'm not close to 'Matt tough.' I'd be an easy target."

"Until we know if this was related to our investigation, you are right, we need to just assume it is and prepare for the worst. It is better to be as safe as possible." He also didn't hate the idea of her in his bed—even if he was to kiss her again. "But I hope you don't think you need to be afraid. I won't let anything happen to you. Ever."

She caught his gaze and smiled so sweetly that it made his heart ache from swelling.

"I won't tell anyone how sweet you really are, okay?" she teased.

"What?" he asked with a laugh.

"You kinda acted all tough around Nicole and Eliot at dinner tonight."

"Oh." The joy fell from him.

"You don't like her, do you?"

He looked out the windshield like he suddenly needed to really concentrate on the darkened roads. He didn't want to tell her about Vince's admission to him about his sleeping with Nicole around the time of Eliot's accident.

"Why don't you?" She clearly didn't have to get a verbal answer for the first.

It was impressive how well she already knew him.

"I can't tell you, but what I know isn't the only reason I avoid her. She has a way of just..." He made a knife-dabbing motion with their entwined hands.

"Oh, I know exactly what you mean. She told me you are still in love with your ex."

He jerked the wheel so hard, they nearly drove off the road. "Are you effing kidding me?" He corrected and slowed down. "Pardon my language. But seriously, no way. I wouldn't have anything to do with her if my life actually depended on it."

"That's what I told her."

"I am over the entire situation. All of it. I'm angry at Nicole for trying to get under your skin and start a problem between you and me, but as for the rest of it with Haven, I'm apathetic. She made her choices. I'm just glad it saved me from having to go through a lengthy and painful divorce."

"Well, that's one way of looking at it."

He shrugged. "Obviously, she never really loved me."

"She made a huge mistake, but if she hadn't, I wouldn't be holding your hand. I guess there's always a silver lining."

"I'm glad for every second I've gotten to spend with you. I was so glad when you came back this morning. Why did you?"

She looked at their entwined hands. "You couldn't help the timing. Fate is funny. I think it was a way for me to take a second and realize that it was okay for me to move on."

He lifted their hands and kissed her fingers. "Tonight can be whatever you want it to be. It's been a long day. If you want to take a shower and just hit the rack, I'd completely understand. I have a great watch list and popcorn."

She leaned her temple against their hands and didn't say anything as they pulled into his driveway and he parked. He kissed the top of her head and touched his forehead to where he had just kissed. The action was so simple, but so filled with love, that he wanted to pull her into his arms and over the console and just hold her to him, but he reminded himself they were almost inside.

She sat up and moved to open the door.

"You wait right there," he said with a smile.

He got out, hurried around to her side and opened her door. "You've worked enough today. Tonight, let's give you the princess treatment." He scooped her up into his arms and kicked the door shut.

Her giggle carried out into the night, threatening to lure the sun up with its warmth.

"I could listen to you giggle forever. Did anyone ever tell you how beautiful your laugh is?" he asked, smiling as he walked her to his front door.

She pulled her arms tight around his neck. "You don't have to be so sweet. You already have me swooning."

"Oh, do I? Was it obvious that I was trying?" He laughed. "I always thought a woman wanted to be swept off her feet."

"I don't know that they meant literally, but I definitely like it. You can do this any time."

"Any time?" he asked with a quirk of the brow. "You promise?"

She giggled and kissed him. It was so unexpected and sweet that he dropped her to her feet so he could hold her in his arms. He loved the feeling of her in his arms, the weight of her and all she represented—love, strength, partnership, and thoughts of more.

Her tongue traced the edge of his lip and he slipped his hand down her back, cupping her ass. He pulled her tight against him with his other, pressing into the center of her back. She gasped at the pressure, and he smiled as he moved his kiss down her neck and then back to her lips.

He was hungry for her; he needed to taste every part of her.

JAMIE HAD BEEN fantasizing about this moment in flashes since she had first met Pierce, not that she would have admitted it to anyone but herself. She loved the way his body was hot as fire against her skin. He wanted to possess every part of her, and she yearned for him to take just as much.

She broke his kiss and took him by the hand. "Let's take this inside," she said, motioning in the direction of the house.

He glanced at the front of his house and then out toward the lake. "You know what… I have a better idea. What do you think about a campfire?"

She put her hands over her mouth and nodded excitedly. "Oh, yeah, that would be so much fun. I haven't had a campfire in a long time. They are so much fun. We can sit out by it, listen to the waves crash on the beach and watch the stars."

He smiled. "You read my mind." He slipped his hand in hers and they made their way into the house.

She liked his place and its quaint charm—even the antique green couch that was far more comfortable than she would have first expected. It was so unpretentious, and it just *fit* him.

"Why don't you grab a blanket from the living room, and I will run outside and start putting together the fire. Give me fifteen minutes, or so, and it should be going." He walked over to her and gave her another kiss, soft and languid, before slipping out the back door.

She walked into the kitchen and stood at the sink, washing her hands and watching him grab a large log. He picked up an ax that was sitting against a boat shed at the side of the property. The way he walked was so strong and self-assured.

He pulled off his uniform shirt, exposing a skintight white T-shirt he was wearing beneath. Her mouth actually began to water. She wasn't sure how, with all the rangers who worked in the park, she had been lucky enough to have him be the one who'd shown up to help.

Then her thoughts moved to Matt. That night when they'd found Anthony.

She shook the thoughts away. Matt was going to be okay tonight...and if he knew she was here and doing what she was doing, he would kick her butt for ruining the night by being all wrapped up being worried about him. She smiled at the thought of her best friend.

There were so many things he would need. But she would be there for him—tomorrow. Tonight was for her and Pierce.

They had nowhere to be. No one to answer to. They were safely tucked away together in his home. Or, as safe as they could be, as they were together.

Together. The word reverberated through her soul.

She embraced the feeling.

There were never any guarantees when it came to the future—her past had taught her that—so she was going to make the most of this night with him and this time. If this was the only stolen time they were granted, she would treasure it and honor it by making it the best night she could.

Jamie watched him splitting the wood, his shoulders pressing against the fabric of his shirt and his core tightening as he swung. He was an incredibly handsome man. She didn't want to, but she finally turned away when he moved to pick up the pieces of wood he'd split and started to place them in a tent shape in the rock-edged fire ring near the edge of the lake.

Walking into the living room, she grabbed a patchwork quilt that looked as though it had been made about the same time the couch had been manufactured, thanks to the orange and green fabrics and gaudy giant flowers complete with brown centers. She remembered her grandmother having these kinds of patterns on her furniture when Jamie had been a kid.

She picked up the blanket but then put it back down on the couch. The last thing she wanted to think about while she was with Pierce and lying out under the stars, was her grandmother, or his. She chuckled at the thought.

Instead, she walked over to the chair in the corner and picked up a plain green fleece blanket that would probably pick up everything on the ground and require several shakings to flip the pine needles loose. It was worth it, and it *was* soft. She lifted it to her nose; it smelled of fabric softener and Pierce.

She loved that smell.

On her way out, she grabbed a couple of beers. She'd be lying if she said she wasn't a little nervous. It had been a while and though she was pretty sure she was ready to take things to the next level, it was still a big step and one there was no coming back from.

There was thick smoke rising up from the fire pit as she walked outside. She'd probably not waited as long as he'd said, but she didn't care. It wasn't that cold of a night, and she had a blanket if she needed it. What she didn't want was to miss another minute with him. If this was their only night together, she wanted to take advantage of every second.

Pierce was squatting next to the fire, making sure the burgeoning flames were getting enough oxygen. They were still the bright orange, not yet hot enough to put off a great deal of heat, but they would give plenty of ambience until then.

She cleared her throat in an attempt to get his attention in the darkness and so as not to surprise him.

He turned and smiled at her. "You can put the blanket there," he said, pointing behind him. "Normally, the wind comes in from the direction of the cabin and rolls over the lake at night. That way, the smoke shouldn't blow in our faces, at least, not too much."

Following his directions, Jamie set down the beers and laid out the soft blanket behind him on what turned out to be a small patch of green grass. She sat and wrapped her arms around her knees in front of her, watching him work.

As he finished up, he came back to her and sat behind her, putting his legs on each side of her body. "Here, lean back," he said, touching her side gently.

She leaned into him, and he wrapped his arms around her body. He motioned toward the constellation in the sky. "See that right there? Those three stars?"

"Yes." She nodded.

"That's the summer triangle. It's made of Vega, Deneb and Altair."

She smiled as he pointed at each of the bright stars.

"Right there—" he pointed at one "—is Deneb. It is in the constellation of Cygnus the Swan." He took her hand and led her finger to the next. "That is Vega, in the constellation Lyra the Harp." He moved their entwined hands to the last of the three bright stars. "And that is Altair in the constellation Aquila the Eagle."

"How did you learn all that?" she asked, turning back slightly to look at his face glowing in the firelight.

He smiled at her and gave her a gentle kiss on her forehead and let go of her hand. "I used to sit out here with my dad at night when I was a kid. We would fish off the dock and he'd tell stories about the constellations to help me learn them. I guess some of them stuck."

"It sounds like you had a really special dad."

He nodded. "I did. I miss him a lot." He pressed his face into her hair like he was kissing the back of her head, but she wasn't sure. "Someday, I would like to do the same thing with my own kid, or kids."

Her stomach clenched a little, but she wasn't sure if it was with nerves or excitement at the prospect of talking about the future. "How many kids would you like to have?"

"I don't know. At least one. I just want a healthy house, full of love and laughter."

She nearly melted. "Me, too. And I want to teach my kids how to ride. It's an expensive lifestyle, but it's a non-negotiable for me. It's something so important to me, I couldn't imagine having a life where my kids weren't involved in it as well."

"I completely understand that." He pushed the hair away from her neck. As he did, the hair tickled her and brought goose bumps to her skin.

"I…" She started, but found it hard to form words as his warm breath caressed her neck. His kiss fell on her soft skin, forcing all thoughts from her mind. "I… I don't remember what I was going to say," she said, her voice airy.

"Good." He reached down for her legs and pulled her around until she was facing him.

She put her legs around him as their lips found each other. He tasted so good, and he smelled of campfire and sweat. He was intoxicating in every way.

What she felt for him wasn't just lust or longing, though she was feeling both right now…she wanted him, badly. Yet she found herself wondering as he kissed her neck if the ache in her chest was love.

She ran her fingers through his hair as he moved his hands down her and cupped her breast as he kissed. She tilted her head back as he squeezed her nipple through the thin fabric of her T-shirt and bra until it was so hard it throbbed.

He reached and pulled her shirt over her head and threw

it onto the ground. He stopped for a moment, looking at her silhouetted by the firelight that radiated warmth off her.

She reached back and unclasped her bra as he sat and watched her. Sending him a seductive smile, she held up the cups as she slipped the straps from her shoulders. When they were free, he reached for her arm holding the bra up and gently pushed it down, and she let her bra fall free of her breasts.

The summer air felt cool on her skin and her already firm nipples grew impossibly harder. He leaned in, drew the left one into his mouth and gently sucked. Her body clenched with want. Reaching for him, she pulled his shirt loose and over his shoulders, exposing his tanned muscles she'd seen rippling against the offending fabric earlier.

His kissed her violently and their lovemaking turned hurried and fevered as they fell to the ground. Pants stripped off. Thrown. She yanked at her panties, fighting them as he pulled off his T-shirt. He lowered his boxers as they sought to reunite their lips.

She crawled on top of him, leading his body to her. Her wetness covered him without his penetrating her and she smiled as she looked him in the eyes and rubbed her body against his hardness. He felt so good pressing against her. He was so close to being inside. One simple movement, one thrust, and his tip would slip between her folds.

She slid forward on his length, reached down and pressed his tip inside her as she looked into his eyes. There was a beautiful ache as he spread her open and she stretched around him. She groaned as she gently moved on top of him, letting her body ease into the pressure of all he had to offer.

He was so much bigger than she had expected.

Pierce took hold of her hips and rocked her body on him, helping her to roll her hips with the action of his body. Their bodies were in tandem with each other, giving and taking, and she felt the tingling of excitement of the initial smaller climax that was her norm.

The sensations took hold of her as she drove harder against him, letting her folds rub against his body and intensify the enjoyment. She slowed her hips as she felt the ecstasy flow through her. Small aftershocks riddled through her body, making her shudder.

"Did you?" he asked, looking at her with a devilish smile.

"Oh, that is only the start, cowboy. I'm not a one-and-done kind of woman." She answered his devilish grin with one of her own as she leaned down and devoured his kiss.

She picked up her speed, bouncing atop him in the night.

He leaned his head back and his eyes closed as he let out a guttural moan. "Oh my God, you feel so good."

She laughed; the sound dark and heavy with lust. "Watch me ride you."

His eyes opened wide, and he looked down at where their bodies connected. He groaned as she kissed his neck and worked her hips, bouncing on him like a jockey.

She could feel him harden inside her. He was close, so close.

"Jamie…" He said her name like it was a wish.

"Give it to me, I want it." She smiled as she sped up.

He called out, the sound carrying like a wild animal in the night. Primal. Freeing. Unforgettable.

She leaned into his ear. "There are some things cowgirls just do better."

Chapter Nineteen

The morning came far too quickly for Pierce's liking, and that was after they had slept well past his alarm and hers and several phone calls of people looking for them. They just hadn't cared. She had checked on Matt, who had remained stable through the night, and beyond that, everything else had waited.

Jamie was lying in bed as he slipped out. Her arm was over her eyes, blocking out the thin light of the sun as she soaked in the last tendrils of stolen sleep. She looked perfect in her naked form. They had made love until the fire had gone out and only the hot, glowing, orange coal was left in the fire pit.

There had been a thin edge of light on the horizon and promises of the coming morning as they had slipped into the house for rest.

He could easily say it had been one of the best nights of his life. She had told him last night that it had been the same for her, but he wouldn't hold her to it. He smiled at the thought and at her as he took one more look at her before slipping out of the room and silently closing the door.

He was an incredibly lucky man.

His phone pinged with a message as he looked out and checked that the fire was dead. Pouring water in the coffee maker, he started a pot and then picked up the device and checked his message. It was Emily. They had pulled video footage from The Mint. She'd sent him an encrypted email with film.

Opening up his email, he had to wait a moment, but it didn't take long for the email to pop up. He pulled up the video.

The video was clear. It showed Matt walking out of the bar, a man Pierce didn't recognize along with him. The man held up some keys, saying something, and then he walked off toward what Pierce assumed was the parking lot.

Matt stood there for a moment and pulled a can of Copenhagen out of his pocket. Opening up the lid, he took out a pinch and placed it in his bottom lip. As he was putting the can back in his pocket, a person wearing a black coat and a black mask approached from the opposite direction, carrying a metal bat.

Matt, with his back turned, didn't see the first blow to the back of the head coming.

He landed on his knees and fell forward, his face hitting the ground and his arms falling limp at his sides. There were splatters of blood on the sidewalk around his face.

The attacker came up and swung the bat, hitting him in the back. Then again in the back of the head, hard. The blood began to seep from Matt's head and pool on the ground around him as the person kicked his body.

The attacker hit him one more time between his shoulder blades. The person looked up in the direction where the man with the keys had disappeared to, and then turned and ran.

Pierce wondered how long the beating would have gone if they hadn't been interrupted by something off camera.

A black Dodge with the ranch's brand pulled around in front of the bar and parked. The man who had left Matt jumped out and pulled out his phone. There, the video ended.

He watched the video three more times, zooming in on the person in black. Based on their body size, which was about the same as Matt's, that made the attacker about six-foot and over 200 pounds.

He assumed the attacker was male, but beyond that, there was not much information. He texted Emily.

Got the video. Thx. What do you make of it?

It didn't take long for Emily to get back to him.

I'm hdd 2 the hospital. They r extubating Matt. Going 2 question him. Meet me there.

He fired back a text.

Okay. See ya soon.

He didn't want to wake Jamie, she had been sleeping so peacefully, and after everything they had been through in the last few days, she needed the reprieve. In all honesty, so did he.

His thoughts drifted to her sitting in front of the fire, her beautiful body silhouetted by the light of the flames. It had been the night of his dreams. Actually, it had been better than anything he had ever imagined.

If he could have things his way, he would only go back in that room to make love to her again.

The coffee steamed and gurgled as it finished brewing. He grabbed a mug, poured himself a cup, and leaned against the counter and stared outside at the place they had first made love. From that moment forward, that would forever be her spot and anytime he looked out at the lake, he would think of her—no matter what the future brought in their lives.

Thinking about the future, he sighed. He was in deep. His heart was hers and he knew there was no way he could tell her. He liked her so much and now it had shifted into the territory of love and longing, but it was too soon and dangerously fast. Given the trauma and volatility of both of their lives, allowing his emotions to get involved was figuratively playing with fire. In many senses, he could be feeling what he was because she was a safe place in the chaos of his life—was what he was feeling trauma bonding?

He couldn't allow himself to overthink it.

Pierce shook his head as if he could shake out the intrusive and unwelcome thoughts.

Sometimes he wondered if there was such a thing as being too emotionally intelligent and aware. Maybe ignorance really was bliss.

He forced himself to watch the video again instead of picking apart his moments of happiness and contentment.

The attacker was wearing black-and-white Hoka running shoes. He didn't know much about the shoes; he'd only seen the brand at the local sporting goods store a few times when he'd walked through. However, seeing them gave him an idea. It was a stretch, but it was a small town, and if the person wearing them had purchased them, maybe there was a record of the purchase.

It was a needle in a haystack, but it was a place to start.

He puttered around, making a little extra noise as he

moved through the kitchen, cleaning up from the night before and starting the dishwasher.

He sent Emily a quick text message about his idea of looking into the shoes. She quickly reminded him that to get any information that they could use in court, he would need to apply for a search warrant.

As it so happened, he knew just the judge who could talk to the federal judge he'd have to send the search warrant through, stating he believed the beating was in connection to the federal case they were currently investigating in the park.

He jogged out to his truck, grabbed his computer and set to work writing out the application. After thirty minutes and some great writing, if he had to say so himself, he sent the application to the federal judge and fired off a text to Judge Donovan to let him know he'd sent the application to the federal judge with the video and a request he make a phone call to get the process expedited.

He had the search warrant signed and in his hands within ten minutes.

That was, hands down, the fastest search warrant he had ever gotten in his life. For the federal government, that was definitely some kind of record.

He sent Judge Donovan and Judge Casper, the federal judge who signed the order, a quick thanks.

Closing his computer, he sauntered back to the kitchen. He had a feeling it was going to be a productive day.

He grabbed a second travel mug and poured Jamie a cup of coffee to go.

Just as he was about to give in and walk down the hallway to wake her, Jamie came out down the hall, dressed and ready to roll. "Good morning," she said, a wide smile on her face. She looked just as beautiful as she had in the firelight.

"You look stunning," he said, walking to her and giving her a kiss before handing her the cup of coffee. "Are you hungry?"

She shook her head. "My abs are sore this morning. I don't know if it's from laughing or from...*other things*." She sent him a guilty grin.

He laughed. "I like knowing it's a toss-up."

"Thank you for last night. I had no idea how badly I needed...well, all of it." She motioned toward the lake and around the house. "And I didn't mean to sleep like that, but, oh man, it was so nice. I hope Detective Monahan isn't upset."

He shook his head. "Not at all. I've been talking to her. You and I actually need to run to Sportsman's Outlet. I got a search warrant for sales records. Matt's attacker was wearing a certain brand of shoe, and I want to look into anyone who may have purchased them. It's a long shot, but the shoes looked relatively new and I'm hoping maybe we can catch a break."

"You do know people buy shoes online all the time, right?"

He nodded. "Yeah. I know, but these are higher-end shoes. Running shoes that, if I was buying, I would want to make sure fit my foot before committing. I'd want to try them on in person."

She tipped her hand, like she was conceding the point.

It DIDN'T TAKE LONG for them to get to the store. Thankfully, the store manager was working, a man named Brent Grant. He was an older gentleman with graying hair and a friendly smile. When Pierce had presented him with the search warrant, he had been more than happy to help.

Now, he and Jamie were standing with Brent and his tech lady in the main office upstairs in the warehouse-style building. The industrial-like complex smelled like solvent, gun powder and leather, and he had to admit it was a great mix—second only to Jamie.

As the tech lady, Traci, set to work tapping on the keys of the computer as she pulled up the sales records for the last year, Pierce sent Jamie a smile. He couldn't help but let his thoughts drift back to memories of last night's fun.

Brent turned to him. "So, can you tell me a little bit about your case? Why are you looking for just this kind of shoe?"

Given how much the small community seemed to know about the Donovan case, he wasn't sure how much fodder he wanted to feed to the gossip fire. But Brent and Traci seemed like great people, and he could give them some tidbits in an effort to advance their search.

"We are looking for a suspect who was wearing these while they committed a crime. They were wearing all black in the camera footage, and this was their only identifiable feature. We aren't even sure if this person was male or female."

Brent waved him off. "Oh, I might be able to help you a little bit there. Those are men's running shoes. Women's have a different color pattern. I would say you are looking for a male. Here, at least, I don't believe we've ever sold a pair to a woman for her use. Traci?"

She was grabbing a few pages off the printer. "You can take a look." She placed the freshly printed pages on the desk so they could all see each of the four pages of sales.

It appeared that since the shoe had gone on sale, the store had sold twenty-two pairs.

"I worked in our shoe department for more than a decade," Traci said. "If you let me see the brand, I could probably give you an estimate on the person's size. That would narrow our sales list down."

He pulled up the video and zoomed in on the attacker's shoes before handing the phone to Traci.

"Do you mind if I zoom this out a little? I need to see the shoe in contrast to the person."

"Do whatever you need." He motioned toward the screen.

Traci tapped and, as she did, she started to get a self-satisfied grin. "This is definitely a male, based on his gait. And he's wearing a size 9 shoe. Which, interesting enough, is actually smaller than the national average for his height." She handed him back his phone with an air of pride.

He was impressed. Brent reached over and gave her a soft pat on her back. "Now, what about sales in that size?" Brent asked.

Jamie pointed to the page on the far right. "There was a pair sold just recently. Here." She put her finger on a transaction record.

Traci stepped next to her and picked up the paper. "Yep. It was paid for with a Visa card. Let me get back on the computer and see if I can get the details." She sat down and tapped away. "First, there have been only three pairs sold that match our description." She pressed more keys as she spoke. "Here we go. Okay." The printer kicked on.

"Did you find out the names of the people who bought the shoes?" Pierce asked.

Traci nodded as she grabbed the paper off the printer

and handed it to him. "Here you go. Do you need me to do anything else?"

He took the page and stared, disbelieving at the name at the top of the list—David Slayton.

It didn't make sense. David had only met Matt on the mountain. What reason did he have to want to beat Matt nearly to death?

Chapter Twenty

Jamie was so confused as she listened to Emily and Pierce talking animatedly on the phone as they raced toward Glacier Park, "running code," as Pierce had called it with his red and blue lights flashing.

She couldn't reconcile why David, the man who had helped to discover Clyde Donovan's body, would have wanted to beat her best friend. Now, it left her wondering if she and Pierce had been wrong about the attacker wanting to send them a message or threaten them about Clyde's murder.

Unless David had had something to do with the murder?

If he did have something to do with the murder? Then why would he have wanted to work so diligently in uncovering the evidence? He and his team had been the ones to find the speed loader. And, if she recalled correctly, he was also the one who'd suggested that they call in the dog handlers to see if they could locate the exact location where Clyde had been killed, or at least decomposed.

It just didn't line up. Nothing about this made sense.

Had Matt had a run-in with David that she hadn't been aware of? Matt hadn't said anything to her about him fighting with anyone to do with the case, or the rescue of Anthony. He would have, if he had thought anything was amiss. He wasn't the kind to hide anything from her. Sure, they hadn't talked a lot in the last few days since the cat attack, not with everything that had happened, but he would have called her with big news.

She checked her phone for messages, even going to all her social media platforms in case she had missed something from him, but Matt had sent her nothing. So strange.

She texted Sally to check on her progress. Sally was quick to text back. She was in Seattle. It wouldn't be long before she was on the ground. From Seattle to Kalispell wouldn't take long. With the layover and flight time, she would be on the ground in two hours.

With the click of a few buttons, Jamie texted her brother to let him know that he would need to pick up Sally at the airport and take her to the hospital to see Matt. He sent a thumbs-up a few seconds later in true brother form.

Pierce hung up his phone and threw it on the dashboard. "Detective Monahan and her team are working another angle," he said, sounding angry.

She wasn't sure she had heard him call Emily "detective" before, and she wasn't sure what had happened during their phone call to make him suddenly be so angered with her, but she didn't like the shift, and it made her feel even more on edge. "Is everything okay?"

He sighed. "We will see. She doesn't think there is validity to Traci's work. I think there is, she is an expert in her field. The other people on that list have no ties to this investigation or the crime."

"Do you think he killed Clyde?" Jamie asked, rubbing her pointer finger and thumbnail together nervously and making a clicking sound.

He looked at her fingers. "I don't know. It doesn't make

sense if he did. He started as a ranger just a short time before the mayor went missing. I don't think he had any ties with Clyde before that as he came out of Dillon—straight out of University of Montana Western with a degree in environmental science."

"How did he get a job in the law enforcement side if he was studying environmental science?" she asked.

"That program works directly with the United States Forest Service, so it's not a big leap. They are just looking for people who are dedicated and willing to work for the government." He gave a dry chuckle.

"So, you don't think there was anything nefarious about his getting a job? Anything which could have led to him having a run-in with Donovan?"

"Short of him screwing his wife—which I don't think, given his short stint here before his disappearance—"

"Do you think David was sleeping with Carey? That he killed Clyde and got rid of his body up here?"

He looked over at her. "I'd be lying if I said the thought hadn't crossed my mind."

She wasn't completely surprised given what she knew about the woman, but before he'd hurt Matt, she would have thought a man like David was well outside Carey's league—that was, unless he had some kind of mother fetish.

In some ways, it seemed too easy.

"Did you ever see David and Carey together? Did he ever talk about dating someone to you?" she asked.

Pierce tapped on the steering wheel for a moment, like the tick helped him to think. "When he was first on the job, he trained with me. I don't remember him saying he had a girlfriend or was in a serious relationship of any sort. We talked about girlfriends and stuff. I remember we talked about my being with Haven, we weren't engaged at that point."

She bristled at the thought.

"He told me that he didn't believe in marriage."

She was confused. "He didn't believe in it?"

He nodded.

Maybe he did have something to do with Clyde's murder.

They pulled to a screeching halt in front of the headquarters. There were several other trucks, just like Pierce's, parked in front.

There was only one other open parking space on the entire street, and it was a stark contrast from the last time she had been at the building with only the patrol captain and the secretary.

Jamie followed Pierce as they rushed inside.

The building, which was filled with empty desks the previous day, was now filled with the comings and goings of officers. The desk in the middle of the room with the nameplate that read David Slayton sat ominously empty.

There was no way David could have known they were coming for him. No one besides the two of them and the employees at the sporting goods store knew what they had discovered. As far as anyone else was concerned, they were still just watching the video and picking at thin threads, hoping to find a decent lead.

Not even Reynolds knew what they had found yet.

She looked toward the office at the far end of the building. It was shut up and dark inside.

Pierce walked toward the office and peeked in through a crack between the edge of the window and the shade. "It doesn't look like Reynolds has been in today." He pulled up his phone. "He is on the schedule and he's not really one for being late. I'm surprised he isn't in."

"Does he drive himself here?"

Pierce shook his head. "We work on government salaries—those kinds of rigs cost a ton of money. I know we have a GoFundMe going for him to get one, but he's not met his goal just yet. For now, Nicole has to bring him in their wheelchair-accessible van."

"Maybe you should give him a call."

"Let me ask if anyone else has heard from him first, I don't want to freak out over nothing." He walked over to the woman they had seen the last time she'd been in the building and started chatting. She couldn't really hear them over the chatter in the building and the clatter of keyboards and phone calls. The woman looked over at her and frowned. She shook her head, and from her body language, Jamie could tell the woman hadn't seen Reynolds.

Pierce came back and motioned for her to follow him outside.

She said nothing as she followed him, but she was dying to know what the woman had said.

As soon as they stepped outside, he looked around and, like he was making sure no one else he worked with was within earshot, he said, "Reynolds called in last night and let his secretary know that he wouldn't be in for the next week. She said she asked why, but he wouldn't tell her if he was sick or what. She said he sounded upset, *off.*"

"I didn't think things went that badly at their house last night. I mean I didn't exactly hit it off with Nicole, but that shouldn't have caused a problem between them. At least, I wouldn't have thought so," Jamie said. "I mean, we got along okay *enough.*"

Pierce shook his head as they got into the truck. "Who knows what's going on with him. It's not like him. Even after his accident, he came back to work as soon as they had him fitted for a wheelchair. He didn't miss a beat. His work is his life. But he may be sick." He shrugged, but there was a worried expression on his face.

Jamie had a sickening feeling in her stomach. Something was wrong.

He tapped on his phone as he drove. "Maybe Emily was right. Maybe it wasn't David in the video."

"If it wasn't him, then why wouldn't he be at work?"

He ran his hand over his face with exasperation. "Right. I know." He exhaled. "We need to find him. That way, at least, we can either eliminate him as a suspect in Matt's attack or find justice."

EMILY HAD SUNK HER TEETH into Carey as a potential suspect in Matt's attack. She just couldn't believe that the attacker was a man based on the gait and that they were men's shoes. According to her, those types of things could be faked or used to throw off investigators.

Pierce didn't completely disagree with her. Carey had some motive to go after Matt. However, he hadn't heard of any connection between the two. In fact, he wasn't even sure that Carey was aware of Jamie taking part in the investigation. Even if she had seen Jamie sitting in his truck while he and Emily were questioning her, Carey wouldn't have had reason to suspect Jamie of any major role, so targeting her best friend from the ranch seemed like a stretch.

That was, unless she was just going after Jamie to get to him. But Jamie hadn't been with Matt, at least not that

Pierce had known of, since they had found Clyde's body on the mountain.

Pierce scratched at the stubble on the edge of his chin as he worked through all the possibilities.

Emily was still at the hospital with Matt, and Pierce didn't want to interfere with her questioning by bringing Jamie there. Emily needed to get as many answers from him as he could provide. However, Pierce would be surprised if Matt remembered much from the attack. From the camera footage, the attacker had come from behind—it was likely he'd never even seen the face of his assailant thanks to the mask, even if he did remember anything about the event.

Pierce tried to call David, but his phone call went straight to voicemail. Pierce told him to call as soon as he got the message. He did the same with Eliot. Then Nicole. It was as if they had all fallen off the planet.

He had no reason to believe the three of them were connected. David worked with Eliot in the same capacity he did, but beyond that, he knew of no deeper connections.

Nothing was lining up.

"What are you thinking?" Jamie asked, almost as if she could read his mind.

Pierce shook his head. "I'm at a loss, but I'm thinking maybe we do need to listen to Emily and look deeper into Carey and her life until we can connect back up with David. It can't hurt. Right?"

Jamie chewed on her top lip. "If we go over there, Carey isn't going to be happy to see you. Did you say she wouldn't speak to you again without her lawyer present?"

He nodded. "She did, but she also wasn't detained at the time she stated that. So, we are free to go to her residence and question her as necessary. She hasn't been Mirandized."

"If she isn't, can anything she tells you be admissible in court?"

He shifted his head back and forth. "Ninety-nine percent of the time the admission will be thrown out. However, if she confesses to something, it makes it a lot easier to hang her up on the stand. Plus, we know where to start to get the evidence we need to prove that she was guilty with or without her confessing if she gets behind a lawyer who keeps her buttoned up."

Jamie gave him a devious look as she nodded. "Then I think we need to go talk to her again. It can't hurt, and then maybe—if Emily is on to something—we can get ahead of it."

He picked up his speed and it only took five minutes to get to the cul-de-sac with the obnoxiously ordinary house. There was a brand-new black Cummins Dodge diesel parked in front of the house that hadn't been there the last time they had been there. The truck was so new, it only had the temporary registration hanging in the back window instead of a license plate.

The truck was lifted and everything on it was top of the line down to the custom deep-dish wheels. It was at least an eighty-thousand-dollar pickup. It seemed out of place in front of the cookie-cutter house with the horrible witch inside.

He really couldn't understand how she had ended up married to a mayor. If this truck belonged to another man, well... He shuddered at the thought.

Apparently, there really was a lid for every pot.

He took a moment to collect his thoughts and plaster on the fakest smile he could muster before he moved to get out of the truck. He started to tell Jamie to stay in the vehicle, but before he had the chance to, she was already out and closing the door. He didn't blame her for not wanting to be left behind, but he didn't like the idea of her coming along.

In reality, though, given how the last meeting had gone with Carey, it was unlikely that they would get anywhere with their questions, so it really wouldn't matter. It was only a fifty-fifty chance that she would even answer the door. She didn't have to—he didn't have a search warrant, and there was no probable cause to come after her in relation to Matt's attack or Clyde's murder.

He was unexpectedly nervous as he made his way up to the door. Jamie walked in step behind him. As he neared the front door, he could hear the sounds of a male and female arguing, and he put his hand down on his sidearm in the holster on his utility belt.

He put his other hand up, motioning for Jamie to stop where she was behind him. "Call 9-1-1, tell them there is a domestic disturbance and I've instructed you to call. I'm Special Agent Hauser with the National Park Service, badge number 406."

She nodded.

"Stay outside. Do you hear me?" He didn't mean to be commandeering, but the last thing he wanted was for her to walk into a hornet's nest and end up getting hurt.

Jamie looked at him with fear in her eyes. "Pierce... Be careful."

He reached back and gripped her hand, giving her a reassuring squeeze. "I will, trust me. You, too. Go back to the truck."

She nodded.

He turned and knocked on the door. "Special Agent Hauser, I'm entering your home!" he yelled. "Put down your weapons and come forward with your hands up!"

His heart thrashed violently in his throat. He dealt with bears, mountain lions and rogue angry tourists, but he had never had to enter a house to stop a partner/family member assault—which was what this sounded like from outside the door.

The screaming from within the house continued. He unholstered his weapon as the door eased open and he stepped inside. He cleared the foyer before walking into the main entertaining area of the house. The man was yelling as though he hadn't heard him announce his presence when he'd entered the building. "You are such a goddamn slut! Why don't you just admit what you did?"

Pierce was careful as he moved smoothly in the well-practiced roll-step used by law enforcement officers throughout the United States.

The last thing he wanted was to walk into a volatile situation and surprise the people in the room—that was how an officer was shot and killed. At least, in a situation like this. Sometimes, an element of surprise was necessary, but not when emotions were running high and weapons may or may not have been in play.

"Carey!" he yelled. "Carey! If you are in here, you need to answer me!"

The screaming continued; a woman was yelling expletives and telling the unknown male where he could go and all the things he could take with him.

Pierce swept the hall leading to the kitchen, clearing the area before making it down to the screaming persons. It sounded like there were only two people, but he'd learned the hard way never to assume. He announced himself again, but the din of yelling didn't change and there wasn't even a pause. It was as if they didn't hear him in the slightest, or maybe they just didn't care.

He pressed his body low against the wall that led into the kitchen, and he could hear Carey and the man shouting about Clyde inside. They were talking about the murder and shooting, and Carey was denying her involvement over and over again. She sounded frightened and desperate. The part of him that despised her didn't feel sorry for the woman, but the honorable civil servant in him felt for her desperation.

"Please," she begged. "I didn't hurt him. I loved Clyde. You have to know I loved him."

"Then why did you file for his death certificate? That isn't something someone does who doesn't have a role in their husband's death." The man sounded so angry that there was almost a whip in his words that even Pierce could feel lash over his skin.

"I needed to get through probate. I had to get things in my name so I could move forward with my life. *You* of all people should understand." The way she spoke made him desperate to look around the edge of the door frame to see the face of the man she was talking to, but if he did, he would be in the direct line of fire if the man held a gun and held a penchant for killing.

"Don't lie to me. I saw the video. And I listen to damn liars every day of my life. You are a fool if you think you can get away with that crap with me." The man gave an angry, dark laugh. "You are just lucky I ever let you live this long."

"Why did you?" Carey asked.

The man's laughter stopped. "Because I held out one last desperate hope that I would find my son alive."

Chapter Twenty-One

Pierce slowly peered around the corner of the door frame and spotted Judge Donovan standing tall over Carey. She was sitting down at the kitchen counter, her hands on the cheap marble surface as she stared up at the man.

He had been right all along. Carey had played a role in Matt's beating—at least from what he'd just heard Judge Donovan allege. She did fit the physical description of the person in the footage, in the loose-fitting black clothes. There must have been some moment when she had put together the pieces and somehow connected Matt to their investigation, but she would have to explain for him to really understand.

Like any breaking investigation, there were always pieces of information that at first didn't seem to make sense or have relevance, but then…*boom,* it all became clear.

There was the metallic sound as the judge slid back the slide and jacked a round into a pistol that Pierce couldn't see, but he knew the sound only too well. He carried a weapon each and every day. He glanced down, instinctively, at the Glock in his hands.

"Judge Donovan, put down your weapon!" he yelled, refusing to step out from behind his cover until he heard the gun hit the ground.

"Who's there?" the man answered.

"This is Ranger Hauser. You need to put your weapon down! You don't need to make this situation any worse by involving guns. Let's talk this out." He noticed a framed painting on the wall across from him of a woman and a dog. In the reflection in the glass, he could see Donovan and Carey in the kitchen.

Donovan looked from her to the gun in his hands. He appeared confused, as if he wanted to put it down and follow orders but was at an impasse with her.

Though he'd trained to always assume the man would remain a threat until neutralized, this was his moment, and he had to act.

Pierce moved around the corner.

The judge dropped the gun onto the countertop. "You know I wasn't going to shoot her. The gun was for my own protection."

"That's good. Just don't touch it. Do you understand?"

The judge nodded. Clearly, he was a man who knew his legal rights and where and what he could do while remaining safely within them and protected.

He could hear sirens wailing in the distance. His racing heart started to slow. The judge didn't seem hell-bent on killing.

"Carey, are you okay?" he asked.

The woman nodded. "I want to press charges."

Of course she does.

"You are delusional if you think they will stick. I have video evidence of you beating Matt Goldstock. You are the one who is going to go to prison," the judge seethed. "I will make sure of it. Don't you know who you are messing with? And that's saying nothing about your role in my son's death."

"I told you," she said, looking between the judge and Pierce, "I didn't kill your son, and I didn't hurt this guy Matt. I don't even know what you are talking about."

"You don't know Matt Goldstock?" Peirce asked.

"No." She shook her head vehemently.

"Where were you last night between the hours of 6:00 p.m. and 8:30 p.m.?" Pierce asked.

"I was with my boyfriend. Mark. He will tell you the same thing. We were here. I promise." She spoke fast. Desperate.

Innocent.

He looked over at Judge Donovan. His face was contorted with rage. "You don't have to lie."

Pierce put up his hand, silencing the angry father. "If I call your boyfriend, right now, would he tell me the same thing?"

She nodded but chewed on her lip as if she was thinking about her answer. "Actually, you don't even have to call him. There are pictures I took of us together last night on Snapchat. I was talking to my friend Jessica. She and I were talking about him."

"What were you saying about Mark?" he asked.

"I have been thinking about breaking up with him." She stopped. "Don't tell him. Please. I don't know what I want in the relationship. Which was why I needed Jessica. I sent her a snap of him talking to me about a fight we were having."

"Can you show me this on your phone?" he asked.

The judge shoved his arms over his chest and looked away. "I can't believe you are listening to this woman. She should be handcuffed, in your vehicle, and on the way to being booked. You know I'm right about her."

He looked at the judge. "Do you remember what you told me the other day?"

Donovan glared at him. "What?"

"Rumors are often true, but they never hold up in court."

"You will never prove anything, I'm telling you." Carey took out her phone and put it on the counter, opening up the videos in her gallery and pushing Play.

They watched as she and a blond man, inside the kitchen where they were now standing, were talking about some kind of fight they were having over moving in with each other. From what Pierce could piece together, Carey wanted Mark to take things to the next level in their relationship, but the man was not having any of it. The time stamp was three minutes after Matt had been attacked at The Mint.

Carey had been telling the truth. She couldn't have been the one swinging the bat and hurting Matt—there wasn't even enough travel time between the two locations.

She was innocent. At least, when it came to beating Goldstock.

"Just because you didn't beat Matt, that doesn't mean you didn't kill my son," the judge countered, but some of the fight had left his voice.

Carey slapped her hands down on the counter, her right hand was millimeters away from the grip of the Glock. "I have effing told you!" she screamed. "I wanted him out of my life. I did. But I'm not a damned murderer." She looked at the gun.

Pierce could see what she was going to do, and time slowed down.

"Don't touch that gun, Carey," he ordered, but as the

words came out in slow monosyllabic sounds, her hand curled around the grip of the weapon.

He raised his gun and aimed it at her.

There was the sound of the front door slamming open and footsteps coming down the hall toward them.

A wave of relief filled him. It sounded as if two people were rushing to help be backup.

The timing couldn't have been better.

Goddamn this woman.

Carey's hand tightened around the Glock, and she lifted the weapon as she pointed it directly at the judge's center mass. "You are just as narcissistic and self-righteous as your son. No one can ever be right but you. I hope you know your son *hated* you."

"He didn't think you were a damned *peach*, either, darling."

He appreciated the judge's tenacity for a good fight, but now wasn't the time to piss the woman off.

The footsteps stopped behind Pierce and he wanted to see who had come to cover him, but he didn't dare turn his back on the gun-toting woman with an anger issue in front of him.

"Carey, I'm only going to ask you one more time. Put the gun down. If you don't put the gun down, you are putting your life on the line. I don't want to have to shoot you."

There was the sound of a woman's laugh behind him and it caught him so off guard that he turned and moved toward the wall.

Standing behind him were Nicole and David.

David stared at him, a deadly look in his eyes. "Just let her shoot him. He came here to kill her. She is within her rights—as long as she shoots him in the front, it's all castle doctrine and self-defense."

"What are you doing here, David?" Pierce asked, turning his body so he could easily see everyone around him.

His skin crawled as he realized he was standing in the death zone if this thing turned into a shootout. There was no worse position for a person to be in. He slowly tried to edge back, but his back was pressed against the refrigerator and there was nowhere for him to escape.

"I'm here to help," David said, a strange, crooked smile on his lips.

"With Nicole? Shouldn't she be outside?" Suddenly, his blood ran ice-cold. Jamie was outside. Had they come here to hurt Carey? Him? Jamie?

What if they had already killed her?

Panic filled him, but if they hadn't seen her, he didn't want to point out her presence to them. He scanned David's clothing; he was wearing the exact same black-and-white Hokas from the camera footage from outside the bar. David *had* been the one responsible for Matt's beating. But why?

He looked at Nicole and she reached over and touched David's arm, the action almost intimate. She was wearing a blue-and-white sundress that seemed wickedly out of place for the moment. Thankfully, neither seemed to have blood on them.

He had to hope Jamie was safe and unharmed.

"Nicole is just fine with me." As David looked at Nicole, it hit Pierce—the two had been sleeping together.

Had Matt seen them together? Was David afraid Matt would out them to Jamie or him? It had to have been why he'd tried to kill. He must have meant to finish the job. But when he hadn't… That was why they were here.

His stomach sank.

They were here not only to kill Carey, but they were also here to kill *him and Jamie*.

They had to make sure no one had seen them together.

There was the sound of a machine and the squeak of tires. He recognized the noise, and he peered around the corner to see Eliot coming down the hall in his wheelchair.

What? Wait.

"You guys didn't have to leave me in the van. I was coming." Eliot sounded annoyed.

David laughed.

Pierce had absolutely no idea what was going on, but he felt deeply threatened. He looked at the judge and at the gun in Carey's hands. She'd lowered the weapon and had it on the counter, still pointed at the judge, but even she seemed at a loss as to what was happening and why these people were in her house.

"Dammit, David. Just get it done," Nicole said. "You're taking too long. If you don't hurry up, the other units may arrive. We can't screw this up."

David turned to Carey and in one swift motion, lifted his SIG Sauer and pulled the trigger. *Tap. Tap. Tap.*

Carey looked at David with shock in her eyes as she peered down at her chest like she couldn't believe what had just happened. Blood started to ooze out of the three holes in her chest, just over her heart, staining her gray T-shirt. She reached up and touched the blood. As she did, her body slumped and she fell forward, falling from the chair with a *thump* as she hit the floor.

Oddly, Pierce didn't feel anything except panic that David would turn and shoot at him next.

Pierce couldn't take the risk and acted before David had

a chance. He pointed his gun at the man who had been his friend. He fired once, hitting the man squarely in the wrist. The gun flew from his hand as blood sprayed violently from the dangerous wound.

Pierce rushed to the gun, grabbing it as David called out in pain and moved to cradle his arm.

Nicole lunged for the gun, but she wasn't as fast. She landed on Pierce. He thrust his elbow back, hitting her in the nose, hard. It made a crunching sound. He could feel the warm wetness of blood on his arm and she pulled back and yowled in pain.

From the corner of his eye, he saw Eliot wheeling toward him with a gun in his left hand and the joystick in his right. Jamie was running down the hall behind him. Taking David's gun, Pierce slid it on the ground down the hallway toward Jamie, hard and fast. "Stop him!"

She picked up the gun as it slid by Eliot, who stopped.

The sirens outside grew louder.

Nicole was crying on the floor beside him as she held her nose. "This is all Eliot's fault. He did it. He killed him." She sobbed. "He killed Clyde Donovan."

In every single scenario in his mind's eye, he'd never ever thought Eliot could have possibly been Clyde's killer. It didn't make sense.

He looked at the gun in Eliot's hand as Jamie walked up beside him and stripped it away without even hesitating. He put his hand up to stop her, but it was too late. She'd already gotten the gun away from him. Eliot moved his wheelchair backward, like he was going to try to escape, but as he did, Jamie reached behind the machine and removed the power cable from the battery.

"She is crazy!" Eliot yelled. "I didn't do anything to Clyde."

"What did you do to my son!" The judge jumped to his feet, but Pierce stood up and pushed his hand into the man's chest, forcing him to fall back and into his seat.

He made sure to keep his gun pointed at David, even though he was sobbing in a heap as blood poured from his arm.

"Pierce!" Emily yelled as she ran inside. "Are you okay? Neighbors reported gunfire!"

"We are in here, Detective!" he called. "We're going to need an ambulance and a coroner." He looked over at Eliot. "Why did you kill him, Eliot?"

Eliot looked from Pierce to Nicole, who was in a heap and crying on the floor. "Before I was injured, I used to care that my wife was unfaithful." He gave a dark laugh. "I caught her in bed with Clyde. I lost it. I shot him in my bed, without a second thought."

Pierce could only imagine the horror of the moment.

"So, you dumped his body?"

Eliot nodded. "I thought the bears would get him long before he'd ever be found. I made a mistake with the speed loader—it must have fallen out of my belt or something when I was dumping him."

Pierce glanced at Nicole. "Why didn't you just get a divorce?"

Eliot scoffed. "I should have, but hindsight... Right?" He looked at his wife.

"He told me he'd kill me if I ever left him...or, if I told anyone what happened that night," Nicole said between sobs. "I never wanted to stay."

"She is lying," Eliot countered. "She has a free ride. I

pay for everything. Then…after my accident, you get even more—don't you, woman?"

Nicole gave a single dry laugh. "I wish you had just died."

"Sometimes I wish the same thing," Eliot said with a sneer, and he looked at Pierce. "Now you can tell, the joke's on me. With me, she has stability, a house and all the money she could want. And now, I have to watch her take lovers and because of my body and my inability to perform as a husband should, I feel like I can't say a damned thing about it. Karma has come full circle. I'm at her mercy. She has to care for me."

Nothing the man had said was justification for what he'd done or the choices he'd made. There were so many other choices he could have made instead of pulling the pin on the grenade that was homicide. If he was stuck in his life of evil, he had done it to himself. He wasn't going to find a moment of pity from him.

Pierce couldn't help the judgmental chuckle that fell from his lips. "Well now, Eliot, you won't need her anymore. From here on out, you will get all the care you need in prison."

Chapter Twenty-Two

The ranch was abuzz with the comings and goings of ranch hands and community members who had been invited for the inaugural Fourth of July picnic Emily and Cameron had decided to put on to help raise funds for Matt and Sally for his recovery.

There was a local band, Shane Clouse and the Dawgs, playing country music from the stage setup in front of the barn. They'd even gotten a dance floor set up and several couples were already out there dancing.

At the edge of the dance floor, Stephanie and Vince were holding hands and chatting with several other rangers from the park. They made an adorable couple.

Anthony Lewis, the man she and Matt had saved, was there. His arm was still in a cast, and he was wearing a patch over his eye, and from what he'd told her, he would need several surgeries. While he had a long road to recovery, he had been grateful for all they had done for him. His girlfriend, Cynthia, had cried when extending her thanks when they'd arrived.

Brent and Traci were there from the sporting goods store and Jamie had recently found out they were married. She'd had no idea when they had been going over the footage, but now it was obvious thanks to the way Brent looked at his wife. She could see the love in his eyes. He was devoted to the woman in a way that made Jamie glance to Pierce and smile.

Almost as if he could feel her gaze, Pierce looked over at her and sent her a wink and a warm grin. She loved him so much.

"You guys are sickening," Matt said, laughing loudly at her as he caught their little wordless exchange.

Ever since he had gotten out of the hospital, Matt had been doing pretty well, but he needed a cane to get around due to the injuries sustained to his lower back. David had done a number on him in his attack.

At sentencing, the federal court had given David twenty-five years for one count of attempted homicide. For his killing of Carey, he'd received life in prison. All his sentences were to be served concurrently in a prison in Arizona.

She felt a little sense of justice in the fact the man would never see mountains again.

Eliot and Nicole had also been given life sentences for their roles in the murder and subsequent cover-up of Clyde Donovan. Nicole was going to do her time in a women's prison in Nevada and Eliot was going to be in California.

The thought of the three murderers and the justice that had been wrought upon them brought a smile to Jamie's face as she looked around at the crowd. Judge Donovan was there, celebrating.

She wasn't sure how she felt about Donovan getting away with his coming into Carey's home and threatening to kill her, but given how everything had played out—no charges had been filed against him and he had walked free.

If Jamie ever had a son, she could understand the man's desire for revenge. He was just lucky he had been saved by

Pierce getting there in time to find out the truth. If Pierce hadn't, it would have been the judge who would have been sent to prison. She couldn't imagine a judge would survive a single day in a prison filled with the men he'd put inside.

Pierce came sauntering over carrying two iced teas. "You doing okay?" asked. "You look like you have the weight of the world on your mind."

She nodded and smiled. "I'm good. Just thinking about how far we've come in just a short time."

He nodded. "I hear you. It feels like we've known each other for years, doesn't it?" He handed her the iced tea. "Two sugars, no lemon, just like you like it." He gave her a kiss on the cheek.

Matt and Sally were sitting at one of the picnic tables and as Pierce kissed her, Matt smiled and waved her over.

She turned to Pierce. "Do you want to go sit with them?" she asked, pointing toward her best friend and his wife.

"Sure." Pierce smiled. "Are you hungry? The hot dogs and burgers are just about ready. Of course, I think your brother is even grilling some steaks. What would you like?"

She waved him off. "I'm okay. Let the guests eat first." She looked over at the grill where her brother was standing with a beer in his hand and chatting animatedly with some people she didn't recognize.

There was a long line of folks at the food table and even more where they had the raffle baskets and silent auction set up. It amazed her how many people had come out in support of the ranch, her family, and her friends. This place had come a long way in repairing their reputation since her father's passing and she couldn't wait to see how far she and her family would continue to take the cattle ranch.

As they sat down, Matt looked over at Pierce. "You

didn't tell her, did you?" he asked, sounding more excited than she had heard him in…well, years.

Pierce shook his head. "This moment is all yours, man. Have at it, but you probably want to grab Emily and Cameron."

Matt turned and waved at her brother and his wife. Emily smiled widely as she spotted them, and she smacked Cameron at the grill. He looked over and he gave them a big thumbs-up. Putting down his tongs, he said something to his friend before he and Emily came sauntering over toward the table.

"What is going on, you guys?" she asked. She looked at Sally. "Are you pregnant?"

Sally tilted her head back and barked a laugh. "Oh gawd no. We need to get things settled first before we jump into that kind of shark-infested water." She looked pretty with her dark black hair that glistened in the summer sun.

It was so good to see her and Matt happy that it almost made Jamie's heart burst.

Cameron flopped down at the end of the table and Emily gently slipped next to him on the bench. "Okay," Emily said, "tell her. We are dying for you to give her the news."

Matt smiled widely. "So, Jamie," he said, looking over at her, "we have all been talking."

"Are you kicking me off the island?" she joked, trying to figure out why they seemed to all be so excited. It was making her uncomfortable.

"Just shut up and listen, sister." Cameron laughed.

"Your brother and Emily have agreed to have it at the ranch, and John's parents reached out and they received some money from his life insurance, and we have all pooled our money together," Matt said. "We started an equine therapy business in your name. Everything you need, as far as the legal and business side is concerned, is good to go. We called it the JMac Foundation, in honor of you and your boy. There's enough money to buy a few horses, do some high-end marketing, and hire some reliable live-in staff at the ranch." Matt pointed between himself and Sally and loudly cleared his throat.

Jamie threw her hands over her mouth in surprise. "Oh my… No… You guys didn't!"

She didn't know what to say. Until now, she'd wanted this but hadn't a clue how she would have been able to make it all happen. To get it up and running like this had to have cost them at least a half-million dollars.

Tears streamed down her face.

Pierce put his arm over her shoulder.

Matt smiled. "It was all Pierce's idea. He was the one who talked to the attorney and got the ball rolling while I was in the hospital. He was even going to get loans until John's parents heard what he was doing and reached out to me. They want you to know they are incredibly proud of you and how you are moving forward with your life."

Her tears intensified. She wanted to be embarrassed for her display of emotions, but she didn't care. She loved these people; everyone at the table loved her. They were her life.

She turned to Pierce. "Thank you, babe. Thank you so much," she said amidst grateful sobs.

He reached up and softly cupped her face between his hands. He leaned in and kissed her forehead. "You deserve everything you want in this life. I love you."

She let the tears run. "I love you, too." She turned to her friends and family. "And I love all of you, too."

"Do it now, brother. Do it now," Cameron said in his low baritone voice.

Pierce shook his head as he looked over at her brother and he dropped his hands from her face. He took her hand with his. "I don't want to take away from this. This is about Matt."

Matt shook his head. "We are best friends, we don't compete. We support each other and we share our greatest moments. Do it, brother."

Pierce got up from the table and moved down to one knee beside her.

She wasn't sure her heart could take any more. That, or she would run out of tears.

"Jamie Trapper, would you do the honor of—"

She threw her arms around his neck and buried her face in him. "Yes!" she exclaimed, not waiting for him to finish and not waiting for him to take out a ring.

None of that mattered. She didn't care about material goods. After all she had lost and all she had gained, what she truly cared about and treasured was in her arms and surrounding them at the table.

No matter what life brought them, they would be grateful for the moments that they were lucky enough to spend together in the bonds of love.

* * * * *